WINNING THE BATTLE

Stephanie Perry Moore
&
Derrick Moore

WINNING THE BATTLE

Alec London Series
Book 4

MOODY PUBLISHERS
CHICAGO

© 2012 by
STEPHANIE PERRY MOORE
AND DERRICK MOORE

Edited by Kathryn Hall
Interior design: Ragont Design
Cover design: TS Design Studio
Cover photo and illustrations: TS Design Studio and 123rf.com

Library of Congress Cataloging-in-Publication Data

Moore, Stephanie Perry.
    Winning the battle / Stephanie Perry Moore, Derrick C. Moore.
        p. cm. -- (Alec London series ; bk. #4)
    Summary: Fifth-grader Alec, frustrated over many things, decides there is no point in trying and begins to sleep in class and spend time with the wrong crowd, but when he starts taking karate lessons to protect himself he learns the value of discipline and conducting himself in ways pleasing to God.
    ISBN 978-0-8024-0414-5 (pbk.)
    [1. Conduct of life—Fiction. 2. Middle schools—Fiction. 3. Schools—Fiction. 4. Bullies—Fiction. 5. Family problems—Fiction. 6. Karate—-Fiction. 7. Christian life—Fiction. 8. African Americans—Fiction.] I. Moore, Derrick C. II. Title.
PZ7.M788125Win 2012
[Fic]—dc23

2011036922

Printed by Bethany Press in Bloomington, MN - 01/2012

1 3 5 7 9 10 8 6 4 2

Printed in the United States of America

To our nephews
Kadarius Moore &
Franklin Perry III

We are so proud of both of you.
God has truly blessed you with
endurance and intelligence.
Though you've learned early that life isn't
always fair, you know God is always good.
If you keep on keeping on and not let
circumstances hold you back, we know
that you'll both keep winning life's battle!

Know also that your uncle and aunt believe
in your brilliant moves . . . we love you.

Contents

Self Defense

1

So the first day of fifth grade is supposed to be *all that*. Right? Wrong! Like all of last year, I'll have to get up super early every day and head off to school with my father.

Let me make this plain. It's not that my dad will just drop me off, because that wouldn't be too bad. What has me so bummed is that, in my case, he'll park in the spot marked "Principal." You see, my father now rules the school. He's over everybody. That puts me in a position to get teased by my peers. And I mean big time.

I guess you can tell this isn't something I want at all. But Dad is super excited about it. Heading to school the first day, all I could do was sit there and listen to him talk about what a terrific year it was going to be. I wanted to throw up.

Last year, when Dad was the assistant principal, a lot of kids thought I was the school pet with special privileges.

Believe me, that wasn't the case. Now that he's been promoted, it's going to be even harder to convince people that I don't get any favors from him.

On top of that, he signed me up to do safety patrol. I'll have to wear this big orange belt across my chest and around my waist. Several cool points gone right off the bat, you think? It's funny because when I was in first and second grade, I sort of thought that having one of those belts and being a hall monitor would be really great.

Now I know it won't be so cool. Since Dad is the principal, it's going to be a no-win situation for me. Everybody's going to think I'm trying to be somebody big if I write them up. Or even worse, I'll lose my job and be in huge trouble with my dad if he catches me looking the other way.

Then, there's another reason why I'm unhappy about school this year. It hit me like a ton of bricks the other day when Dad started naming some of my classmates. Right away, I knew it was bad news for me.

A lot of kids don't want to be in a particular teacher's class. But in my case, I'm okay with my fifth-grade teacher. After all, Dr. Richardson is known as the coolest teacher in the whole school. It was even cool to find out that Morgan, Trey, and Billy are in my class again.

The problem for me is that I didn't shake Tyrod. Besides that, his equally troublemaking buddy, Zarick, is in my class too. I don't want to deal with them. But after much pleading with Dad, it looks like there's no escape.

All of last year, Tyrod was the person who got under

my skin. Just to cause trouble for me, he made up stuff and got me sent to my dad's office several times. He even tried to cheat off my paper and then turned around and said I tried to cheat off of his. It was just one thing after another with that guy.

In my defense, I get along with most people. Yeah, I had to get over being angry and acting like a bully when I was in the second grade. But that was years ago. I've grown up a lot since then. However, with Tyrod and his friend constantly getting into all kinds of trouble, I just don't see how it's going to be a good year.

When Dad and I arrived at school, he was still going on and on in a happy mood. As we were getting out of the car, he said with a big smile on his face, "Oh yes, it's going to be a great year!"

All I could do was look at him and beg, "Dad, pleeeeesssss change my class!"

As we walked toward the door, he started giving me all these reasons why he wouldn't. But it just wasn't what I wanted to hear at that moment. "Alec, son, we've been over this already. Ever since you found out that your name is on Dr. Richardson's class list, you've been complaining. I know you're going to love her. She's a lot of fun and really knows her stuff. You're in the fifth grade now. You know you need to pass the CRCT like you did in the third grade. This year, it's a crucial exam for you, Alec, and I can't—"

"Dad! Dad! You're not listenin' to me! It has nothin' to do with Dr. Richardson. I just don't want to be in—"

Cutting me off, he said, "No, son, you're not listening to me! I'm not changing your class because of some other student. If you have a problem with Tyrod, you let me know, and I'll deal with it."

I shook my head and turned the other way. I wasn't trying to be disrespectful to my father, but he didn't get it. I couldn't just run to him and tell on people. Yeah, I know there's some stuff you're supposed to speak up about. But this isn't a life or death situation. Besides, I'm not a wimp, and I don't need my dad to fight my battles.

Once again, Dad made it clear that he wasn't going to change my class. So the only thing left for me to do is man-up and deal with it.

A few minutes later, I took my post by the front door. Standing across from me was Gilmer, a boy from my fourth-grade class. Last year, he was the new guy and didn't say much. But he did tell me once that he was cool with not having friends. So I already knew that Gilmer was very shy and didn't like talking to people.

If he was going to be my partner, I was thinking that we wouldn't have much to say to each other. Then, to my surprise, I found out something different when Gilmer spoke to me.

"Hey, Alec! Hope you had a great summer!"

Wow, is this the same Gilmer? I thought. He sounded so happy and friendly.

"You're talkin' to me?" I said to him.

"I know what you're thinkin', Alec, but I've changed.

I'm older now. I guess it took me a while to get comfortable with this school, but now I just wanna enjoy my fifth grade year. I wish we were in the same class because I think we could have a lot of fun. Maybe we can do that while we're on safety patrol duty. You okay with that?"

"Yeah. That's cool with me. We can be friends," I said to him, still shocked at the new, talkative Gilmer.

Okay, so now it seemed like everybody was ready for fifth grade—except me. Then, in a flash, I was reminded of why. I watched Tyrod and Zarick running toward the front door when they got off of their bus.

"Hey! Hey! Slow down," I said to the two of them, holding my arm out to block the doorway. I wasn't supposed to let anyone run into the school.

"Boy, you'd better get your hand back outta my way!" Tyrod said to me.

"Boy, you'd better slow down!" I quickly responded back to him.

"And if we don't slow down?" Zarick stepped up and added, looking and acting all tough. He is taller than me and a little intimidating.

"Yeah, what you gonna do?" Tyrod jumped up and down in my face, asking me.

It was clear to me that they weren't going to cooperate, and I knew this wasn't going to be pretty. Seconds later, Gilmer left me and I had to stand my ground alone. Other kids were coming into the school, and they were looking at the whole scene. If I was going to be good at safety patrol, I had to stand tall. Otherwise, kids would think I was a pushover. At the moment, the only thing I could think to do was take out my safety patrol merit notebook and wave it in their faces.

Before I got a word out, Tyrod said in a lower voice, "We'll stop runnin', but you'd better watch it!" He kept looking over my shoulder the whole time.

I wondered why Tyrod calmed down so quickly. Then I turned around to see what he was looking at. That's when I saw Gilmer coming up behind me, along with my dad. It was cool that Gilmer was trying to have my back.

My father spoke right away. "Is there any trouble here, boys?"

Gilmer nodded and Zarick backed away from me. But Tyrod got closer to my ear and whispered, "Go on and cry to Daddy. You'll be sorry."

Tightening my jaws, I said, "Naw, everything's fine, Dad. I was just tellin' them to slow down."

My father said to the two troublemakers, "I know you boys weren't running, were you?"

"No, sir," Tyrod said in a most respectful tone. Zarick just shook his head.

"Tyrod, we're going to have a good year. Right?"

Faking it again, he replied, "Oh, yes. A great year, sir, a great year."

After that, Dad allowed Tyrod and Zarick to enter the building. He told everyone else to hurry on to class.

Finally, my post for safety patrol was done, and it was

time for me to get to class too. The teachers had already cleared the hallway of their students. As I headed around the corner, I picked up my pace so I wouldn't be late. Then, out of nowhere, I got tripped. Suddenly, I was on my back. All I could see were hands moving at lightning speed, chopping at the air—right in front of my face. It was happening so fast that I wasn't sure what was going on. It was like something out of an old Bruce Lee movie that my brother, Antoine, and I love to watch.

After blinking my eyes a couple of times, I realized it was Zarick. He was acting like some type of karate expert. Then he leaned down and said, "Tyrod and I can do whatever we wanna do. Remember that."

Next, Tyrod leaned over me and said, "And if you tell anybody about this . . . those moves that scared you right now . . . next time, they'll hurt you." Then he pointed at Zarick and said to me, "You might think you're tough and can fight, but you don't want any part of him. You can't protect yourself, little boy, so don't get in our way."

Through blurry eyes, I looked at both of them, too scared to get up or try to move. As they walked away snickering, it only took a minute for me to go over what just happened. It was pretty clear that Zarick had real skills, and I wasn't planning on challenging him. But at the same time, being scared all year long didn't sound so great either.

I just lay there a couple more minutes, thinking, *How am I gonna defend myself against the two of them? I knew this year wasn't going to be good the minute I found out we were in the same class.*

● ● ●

"Well, you must be Alec London," the smooth-talking, short lady said with a big smile. She was wearing a nametag that read DR. RICHARDSON.

I didn't want to be rude to her, but I'd just been through an experience that still had me frazzled. I wasn't ready for any conversation. So I nodded to let her know that she was right.

As I tried to get by her, she put her hand on my shoulder and walked me back into the hallway. "Why the long face?" she asked. "This is going to be a super great year! You know, supercalifragilisticexpialidocious!"

I looked at her like I didn't understand.

"Alec, you know that word is from the movie *Mary Poppins*, right?"

"I'm sorry, ma'am, but I've never seen that video."

She went on talking. "Oh, you're missing something great. I'll make sure we watch it before the year is out. But again, why the long face? I just have to say, Alec, I know it's got to be tough having your dad as the principal of this school. I can't solve the world's problems, but if you have any issues, I want you to know that you can come to me. Mr. Wade and I talked about some of the incidents that occurred last year. However, I'm telling you now that I don't tolerate foolishness."

It was okay for her to let me know that she had my back. But again, I didn't want anybody handling things for me. It's like what Gilmer told me last year when Tyrod and four of his friends tried to gang up on him. I stepped in to help Gilmer, but he didn't seem to appreciate it. That offended me until I understood that he never asked for my help. I kind of wanted to say to Dr. Richardson that I wasn't asking for hers either.

Knowing that wouldn't be the right thing to do, I just tried to smile instead. She was a smart lady and seemed to understand my problem. Dr. Richardson then said to me, "Alec, I get that you're a fifth grader and you don't want to run to the teacher for every little thing. However, I just want you to know where I stand. I'm here for you."

"Is it because you don't want my dad to think you wouldn't help me?" I asked her.

I was thinking that maybe she wanted to score some brownie points with my father. After all, her title is "Dr." Richardson. It seems to me that most doctors in education would want to be a principal, a superintendent, or something like that. Most likely, she was trying to help herself by helping the principal's son.

My wise teacher looked at me and said, "Okay, so you do want to talk. The reason I want you to be able to open up to me is because I've walked in your shoes."

I gave her another confused look. "I don't get it."

Dr. Richardson explained, "My mother was the principal of my elementary school. So I know firsthand about all the stuff someone in your shoes has to go through. Therefore, in addition to teaching my class, part of my role as an educator is to create a safe and healthy learning environment. I wouldn't be doing my job if I didn't let you know that you can talk to me if you have an issue. However, it works both ways with me. If you do something wrong to anybody in my class, and you don't act like the upstanding young man that everyone says you are, then you and I will have problems. I don't play favorites. I only reward excellence. Is that clear?"

I nodded at her that I understood. Finally, she said, "Now, I have something to take care of, and I'll be back in a few minutes. The class is in there getting to know each other by working on a puzzle that I passed out. There's one on your desk, so get in there and start mixing. And remember our discussion. Okay, Alec?"

"Yes, ma'am."

As I walked into the classroom, everyone looked at me as if I had something like the mumps, the measles, or the chicken pox. I knew it was because my dad is the principal and a lot of kids aren't sure how to treat me. Thankfully, Trey and Billy called out to me.

"Hey, man! I'm glad to see ya," Billy said. "We're in the same class again. That's so awesome!"

Without any excitement, I replied back, "Yeah, it's cool." I know that Billy likes to eat, but I was surprised to see how much bigger he was since last year.

Next, Trey jumped in, "Hey, man. My dad said it would

be okay to have you come to a Falcon's practice with me soon. You have a good summer?"

Hearing that news, it was hard to hold back a smile. "That sounds real good, man," I responded. Trey reminded me of some good times, so I added, "Yeah, summer was cool. I went to California to stay with my mom."

"What? You mean, you were in Hollywood?" Trey asked, reaching out to give me a fist bump.

"Yeah," I said, pointing my fist toward him.

Billy jumped in and added, "Oh yeah, people said they saw you on TV. Were you really?"

"Just a little public service announcement that ran on the PBS channel. No biggie."

"Wow! My friend is a star," Billy said with a proud grin. Tilting his head toward one corner, he said, "Those girls over there keep lookin' at you."

I glanced over and saw two girls I'd never met before. They were giggling and quickly turned away.

Just then Morgan came up behind me and said, "Hey, Alec! They're giggling because they like you."

"So? I don't like them," I shot back real fast.

She teased me and said, "Already, they won't be my friends because you like me."

Frowning at that, I said, "Who says I like you?"

Morgan looked embarrassed and responded softly, "I only meant as a friend."

As soon as she walked away, I realized that I'd hurt her feelings. I wasn't trying to be mean to her. But I'd never told anyone I liked her, so I couldn't help but react. Still, the way it felt when she was across the room looking sad, I wished I could take back those words.

A minute later, Billy headed back to his desk. As he stooped to sit down, Tyrod pushed his chair away from him and Billy fell to the floor. When laughter broke out around the classroom, Trey and I just looked at each other. We didn't think it was so funny.

By the time Dr. Richardson came into the room and explained the next assignment, Tyrod had already gotten to me. The teacher passed out bingo cards and told us we had to find the right person in the class to match each square. I got Trey to initial the one that said to find a good friend. Billy signed the one that said to find someone whose favorite hobby is eating. I asked Morgan to sign the one that said to find someone who has a younger sibling.

Once you got somebody to sign one square, they couldn't sign anymore. For me to have bingo, I had two more boxes to complete. One asked, "are you a ballerina?" and the other asked, "are you a girl?" I thought about the two girls who were looking at me earlier. I knew at least one of them would probably sign for me.

Just as I was walking toward them to ask, I heard a loud bump and someone yell out. I looked back and saw that Trey had fallen on the floor. I then noticed that his shoelaces were tied together. Zarick and Tyrod were huddled together, grinning real hard. I figured it was their way of telling the class that they owned the room and dared anyone to say anything.

Dr. Richardson gave the class a stern warning, telling us she wouldn't allow any misbehavior. In frustration, I stopped playing the game right then and sat down.

Seconds later, Tyrod jumped up and called out that his card was full. He was the winner. Someone could have knocked me over with a feather.

At lunchtime, I got my tray and found a seat. Trey came and sat next to me. He was pretty upset about what happened to him in class. "That boy Zarick knows karate," Trey started. "But I'm not gonna be pushed around. I'm gonna tell my dad that I want to take karate lessons. I'm gonna find a way to deal with him."

That was an interesting thought. I had to be able to defend myself too. Karate, huh? If Zarick knows it, maybe I need to learn it too. And if I work twice as hard, maybe I could catch up to his level pretty quickly. I mean, he couldn't be as good as a black belt. But one thing is for sure—he's pretty scary.

Trey had given me a great idea. I wasn't going to be frightened anymore. I could learn karate and beat Zarick at his own game. Hmmm, now that sounded real exciting to me.

● ● ●

"So Dad, what do you think? You just finished talking to Trey's dad. Can I go to karate class? It'd be good for me, right?" I asked question after question, trying to find out what Dad's answer was going to be. For some reason, he wouldn't give me one.

My father just hung up the phone, huffed a little, and walked away. I followed him and asked even more questions, but he still wouldn't respond. He didn't say whether I could go to karate or not. He said nothing at all.

"Daaaaaddddd!!" I finally shouted.

"Look, Alec, calm down. You know that I don't play games. You put me on the phone with another adult when I had no idea what it was about. Don't ever ambush me like that to get a yes out of me. It won't work."

"No, no, Dad. That's not it. I was just talkin' to Trey, and he was sayin' that his dad wanted to talk to you, and . . ."

"His father didn't want to talk to me. He didn't even know what it was all about. You and Trey are in the fifth grade. You're too old for silly first-grade behavior. If you want something, come to me and ask me. If I need more information, then I'll find it out. The man started talking about how much it costs as if I couldn't afford it. It was just uncomfortable. Don't do that anymore."

"Yes, sir," I said, bowing my head.

"So I can't go?" I asked him.

"You wanna do karate?" Antoine said as he came out of the bathroom after listening to our talk. "I could teach you karate. Come on over here and let me school you with a few cool moves."

My brother started dancing all around me and waving his hands like a chicken flapping his wings. He had no karate skills and couldn't teach me anything, but there was no telling him that. I just stood there and looked at him.

"Don't play. You know I got skills," Antoine said to me. When he finally realized I wasn't paying him any attention, he backed off and left us alone.

"Daaaddd, can I go? Please? I'm sorry I didn't just come and ask you. But I don't ask if I can participate in much. I'm always doing what you and Mom want me to do. I even tried new things like baseball and acting. Now, I wanna try karate. Please?"

"All right, son, I'm going to take you so we can check it out. Actually, the instructor goes to our church, and I respect him a great deal. So maybe it'll be good for you."

"Who at our church knows karate?" Antoine called out from his room.

"Kids call him 'Stone' because that's his last name. At one time he was a boxer. Now he gives karate lessons."

"Oh, that man. I hear he's real mean," Antoine said, as he came back into my room. "His daughter's in my class and most of the kids are scared of her. People say she gets it from her dad. I wouldn't want to take karate from him."

Quickly, I said, "Well, you're not me. It can't be that bad."

Shrugging his shoulders, Antoine responded, "Don't say I didn't tell ya."

Two hours later, I was at Mr. Stone's martial arts center,

getting fitted for my karate outfit. When he and Dad finished talking, my father came into the dressing room and said, "Son, I'm going to warn you right now. Mr. Stone doesn't play. He told me if he finds that you're not serious, he'll stop your lessons. Besides that, I won't get a refund on that suit . . . so are you sure you want to do this?"

I nodded.

"Boy, you can speak up!"

Clearing my throat, I said, "Yes, sir. I want to do it."

"All right then, don't come whining and crying if he's tough on you."

Why my father thought I was such a baby got to me. But I figured my actions would speak louder than any words I could say. So I was determined to show him that I could handle this. Before we said good-bye, he told me he'd be back to pick me up in an hour and a half.

When Trey came through the door, it made me feel a little bit better. If Mr. Stone was as strong as everyone said, then at least it would be good to have my buddy around. We could support each other.

"This is gonna be great!" Trey said, while he was getting dressed.

I was standing outside the curtain, listening to my friend and getting more excited. "We'll be able to show Zarick he's not the only one with karate moves. We'll chop him with our hands and bring him down with our feet—"

Just before Trey could finish his sentence, Mr. Stone walked up with a serious look on his face. He reminded me of my father when he wasn't in a playful mood.

"I hear a whole bunch of talking over here! You boys should be out on the floor warming up."

In a flash, Trey pulled back the curtain and hid behind me.

Mr. Stone was a big, tall man, who looked as strong as any super hero. Not only did he have a reputation for being mean, he looked mean. He wasn't smiling, and his eyes were squinted like he was really checking us out.

"I want to see both of you! Step out on the floor, now!" he growled.

I was really nervous and started talking fast. "I'm ready, sir, to learn all you can teach me. I'm really committed to this. I need to be good at karate like yesterday. There's this boy at our school who knows karate, and he's been torturing people. Trey and I figure, if the two of us learn karate, we'll be able to show him that we can take care of anybody."

Then Trey peeked from behind me and jumped in. "Yeah! We'll be the baddest! I mean, you know what I mean, sir?"

"Boys, sit down on the floor!" Mr. Stone barked in a really harsh tone. "You've got the wrong idea if you want to learn martial arts so that you can hurt someone. If that's what you want to do, I'm not going to be the one to teach you. This skill is not intended to harm others. If anything, it's for you to use as self-defense."

Letter to Mom

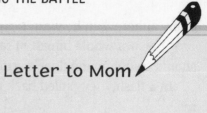

Dear Mom,

What a first day at school! Being the principal's son is going to be difficult. I don't even want any special privileges. That would only make my life at school even harder.

I'm trying not to whine all the time, Mom, but this is a lot of pressure. I want to be judged on my own merit, not my dad's. I don't need people staring at me like I'm always under a microscope. I know I sound frazzled, but I'm trying to avoid having any incidents.

Mom, I need to know how to defend myself. Would you be okay with me taking karate lessons in case I have to beat someone up? I'll tell you all about it in my next letter.

Your son,
Wanting to be tougher, Alec

Word Search:
Parts of the Body

```
M   Z   T   U   A   E   I   A   M   H   F   A
A   T   A   M   A   S   J   B   A   P   D   P
Q   X   S   J   K   T   H   N   U   A   B   Z
X   M   L   G   T   A   A   I   R   K   P   N
C   V   Y   R   F   V   Y   A   S   I   I   N
F   O   M   Q   J   O   K   J   O   B   T   L
Q   E   K   T   E   K   O   Z   U   A   E   K
C   P   C   Z   M   H   U   S   A   R   M   C
V   D   H   P   L   G   L   U   E   E   P   I
N   D   P   N   U   V   S   T   J   N   I   O
T   G   W   Z   K   U   S   F   M   I   E   W
Z   A   X   O   I   W   V   I   J   I   H   N
```

Atama (ah-tah-mah): head
Ashi (ah-she): foot and/or leg
Empi (em-pee): elbow
Hana (hah-nah): nose
Hiji (he-gee): elbow
Karada (kah-rah-dah): body
Kubi (koo-bee): neck

27

Deep Secret

2

Was I hearing Mr. Stone correctly? Did he mean he didn't want to teach us karate? That couldn't be the case. I looked over at Trey, and Trey looked back at me. We were both confused. We have to be taught these skills. Mr. Stone had to understand. We were fifth graders, and we didn't even feel safe in our own school.

Even though he was pretty scary, I said, "Mr. Stone, please wait. You've got to hear us out. We need to learn martial arts, and it is for the right reasons. This guy named Zarick can do all sorts of stuff, and he's being influenced by this tough boy named Tyrod . . ."

"And I think he's teachin' Tyrod some moves too," Trey cut in and said.

I nodded my head. "That's why we need to defend ourselves. We wanna learn from you because we hear you're the best."

"Whenever he gets a chance," Trey added, "Zarick uses his martial art skills. He does all kinds of karate moves and tries to hurt people. So it will be self-defense. But we can't stand up to him if we don't know how to do the same moves that he does. You've gotta help us, sir."

"Young man, I don't have to help you do anything. Besides, you're only in elementary school. It's hard for me to believe what you're saying. Alec, isn't your dad the principal of your school? It can't be an environment that's so terrifying. I'm certainly not going to help you learn what I hold as dear and precious so you can physically assault someone. Whether you think they deserve it or not, you have no authority to decide."

Really needing Mr. Stone to understand, I tried again to explain. "Sir, it's like in the movie *Karate Kid*. If you could just see the bullying, then you'd understand."

Just then Dad came in. Mr. Stone threw up his hands and walked over to my father. Actually, he stormed over to my father. We hadn't been able to convince him, and he was quite upset with us. Trey looked as if he were about to cry.

We were both thinking about how we were going to handle Zarick. "What are we gonna do now?" I asked.

Trey was quick to speak. "I'm gonna find another instructor. That's what I'm gonna do. This time I won't tell him why I want to do karate. I have to learn this stuff, Alec. Zarick is not gonna make me petrified to go to school. It's just not right and it's not gonna happen. I'm not that same scared little second-grade boy anymore. I'm done with all that, and I'm not going backward."

"All right, do you have to keep rubbing it in my face?" I said it a little salty because I was already disappointed in the fact that Mr. Stone didn't understand us. Now my friend was trying to make me feel bad because years ago I was just like Tyrod and Zarick, always bullying people around. However, that was then, and this is now. I wasn't about to let Trey get me down.

"I didn't say it to mess with you," Trey replied, after he saw that he'd made me a little upset. Then he explained, "Alec, I was talkin' to myself. Besides, even though you've changed for the better, I'm still gonna remember. Second grade was hard, then I kinda got a break in third grade. But with Tyrod around, last year wasn't all that good. I definitely want to have a better time this year. I'm not a football player like you. Nobody thinks I'm cool."

Before I could say anything, Trey kept on talking. "I mean, I'm around football players all the time, pro players at that. I really hope that I get bigger and stronger soon. Remember that running back you met last year? He told me, when he was my age, he was the smallest guy in his class. But he had heart and started working out. He worked hard and didn't take any mess off of anybody. That's how he got to the level he's at, and I guess I just wanna do the same."

"I don't look at you as a wimp, Trey."

"Sometimes I feel like a wimp. Like when I hid behind you because Mr. Stone looked like a grizzly bear who wanted to bite our heads off and stuff. I've got to get tougher. If this man doesn't wanna teach us karate, then I'm gonna find somebody who does."

Trey's cell phone started to ring. It was his dad calling to say that he was waiting outside.

"I've gotta go. See ya tomorrow."

I replied, "All right, man, I'll see you later."

Then my friend was gone. It was actually pretty cool talking to him, both of us getting out our real feelings. I wasn't upset with him. He didn't want me to feel bad. He was just keeping it real. I had to own up to the fact that I did hurt him years ago. Yeah, times have changed, and he's forgiven me. But even though we've moved past it, it's still a part of him.

"Alec, come on, son. Let's go," Dad said to me in a tone that let me know he was a little irritated with me.

As soon as we got in the car, he confirmed my suspicion.

"Just so you know, Mr. Stone said you're not ready to learn karate right now."

"Ah, Dad, he's just trippin'."

"Son, slow down and be respectful. Mr. Stone is an adult, and he's also an expert. He knows when people want to learn moves that can be extremely dangerous for the wrong reasons. That's why he refuses to teach you right now."

Knowing my dad never likes to waste a dollar, I said, "But you paid, Dad."

"He gave me my money back and even told me you

can keep the suit until you're ready."

"Are you serious? Take me back in there, Dad. I can convince him that I'm ready now. I've gotta do this."

"Why do you think you have to do this, Alec?" my father bluntly asked me. Then he said, "Talk to me, son. Mr. Stone was telling me some very disturbing things about what you think is going on in your class. If Tyrod and Zarick are using martial arts skills to terrorize other students, then I need to know this so I can take care of it."

Looking out the window and watching the sky getting darker, I said, "Dad, I'm not a tattletale, okay?"

"Alec, you are a safety patrolman for a reason. You're growing up, and I trust you. Why won't you tell me if it's so bad? I'm raising you to do something to make the world a better place—not just to stand by and look the other way."

When he said that, I started to let it all out. "Well, that's what I'm tryin' to do. I'm tryin' to handle it my own way. I am growing up, Dad. I already have enough pressure on me. I'm the principal's son, and all the teachers want to impress you. Of course, they're gonna be extra nice to me. You don't understand. Please, Dad, I don't even wanna talk anymore."

"Son, it really disappoints me that you don't want to open up. We need to talk it through so that I can help you and give you a better idea on how to handle all this. Treating violence with violence is the wrong way. Deep down inside you know that."

Then, he reached over and placed his hand on my

shoulder, as if to say everything was going to be okay. I just looked out the window again and prayed, *"Lord, why doesn't my father understand what's going on with me? Why does life have to be so hard? Trey isn't the only one who needs to get tougher. Mr. Stone won't help me. I need You to make me strong. Do You hear me, Lord? Are You going to help me? Please?"*

● ● ●

On Saturday morning, I woke up with a huge smile on my face. Yeah, it had been a tough first week of school. My father and I had gotten into it, and I wasn't quite sure if I was going to like the fifth grade. Dad wanted me to be tough, a big guy, and talk to him about everything. But he didn't really get me at all.

Today, I have something to be happy about. My mother's coming home for a visit and that's certainly worth looking forward to. Although it hasn't been long since I've seen her, two weeks was long enough. After all, I'm still Mom's baby boy. Of course, I meant it when I told my dad I was growing up. I know that I'm not a baby anymore. But somehow being in my mom's arms and venting to her just seems different.

The house phone rang, and I could hear Antoine shouting, "Get it! It's for you!"

He knew that because Trey's name popped up on the screen when he was watching TV. I picked up right away.

"Hey, Alec!" Trey said in an excited voice. "Hope it's

not too early to call you on a Saturday morning. My dad found another karate teacher and he's gonna take me. I wanted you to know that he can swoop by and get you too."

I sprang to my feet. I looked right in my closet where my uniform was hanging. It was practically new, without a mark on it. I couldn't wait to put it on and get it dirty. Then, just as I was about to rush out of the door and yell for my father to get the phone, I remembered something.

"Wait, wait. My dad's not gonna go for this. He doesn't know anything about another instructor. He doesn't want to be put on the phone with your dad just because I tell him to pick it up. I got in trouble last time. I can't do it, man."

"All right, well, you go and talk to him. The guy's name is Mr. Black. He's supposed to be just as great as Mr. Stone," replied Trey.

"Besides, I can't go because my mom's comin' in today."

"But it's early. What time is your mom supposed to get there?"

"I dunno exactly. Sometime this afternoon."

"We'll have you back home by then. Go ahead and ask your dad, then call me back."

"I just can't ask my dad right now."

As soon as I said that, Dad was standing at my door. He must have heard Antoine shouting at me to pick up the phone. "Ask me what?" he said.

I turned around with my mouth hanging open, but no

words came out. I didn't know what to say.

"Ask me what, Alec?" he demanded.

In a low voice, I responded, "If I can go to karate class with Trey."

"You know Mr. Stone is not going to teach you right now. Maybe we'll try again next month. But you need to let him cool off for a while."

"No, no, Dad. Trey's dad found another place."

"Is that Trey on the line?"

"Yes, sir," I said feeling like I had a chance after all. I could almost see myself learning the moves.

However, my father frowned and said, "Boy, hang up. Right now."

In a disappointed voice, I said, "I'll call you back, man." I put down the phone and then looked at my dad. "Yes, sir."

"I know Mr. Stone. He goes to our church. I feel comfortable with him teaching you karate. Besides, he's got a good point. He thinks that you don't want it for the right reasons, and I agree with him. I'm not going to just let you hop from one instructor to the other. You've got to learn to get on the right page with someone who has your best interests at heart, not somebody just trying to make a quick dollar. That might work for others, but you're going to wait until Mr. Stone thinks you're ready."

That wasn't at all what I wanted to hear, and right away I got upset. "But Dad, that's not fair!" I shouted.

My father didn't look like he cared whether I thought it

was fair or not. "If you're going to get an attitude about it then you're going to stay in this room all day."

Thinking he may have forgotten, I reminded him, "I can't stay in my room all day. Mom's coming."

After taking a deep breath, Dad said, "Son, she needs you to call her."

"What? I don't understand."

Dad looked away and said, "Just call her."

Again, he let out another long sigh.

"Isn't she supposed to be on her way to the airport by now?" I asked. Suddenly, I was having a funny feeling inside me that she wasn't coming.

"No, she's got an early rise this morning. If you're going to catch her, this is the best time."

Okay, maybe she was coming. Maybe that meant she was about to take an early plane and I wouldn't be able to reach her for a while. So, wanting to think positive about it, I quickly dialed the number. I just knew Mom wasn't going to let us down. She was the one who said she was coming every two weeks. Why would Mom say that if she wasn't going to do it? But if she was about to let me down, it would be devastating. Mom couldn't be going back on her word. Or, could she?

She picked up right away. "Is this my Alec on the line?"

"Yes, ma'am, it's me."

"Sweetheart, you know Mom loves you. Right?"

Already, I didn't like how the conversation was going.

"Yes, Mom. I know you do. Please tell me you're still

comin'.'" I jumped right to it and said.

"I want to be there, baby, but—"

Cutting in without letting her finish, I said, "Mom, you're not comin'?"

"Calm down, Alec. Let me talk to you. Let me explain."

"What? It's the job again? They want you to shoot something? Is it a promo? Do you have to do some marketing? I've heard it all. Remember, I've been there with you. Things got moved around again? I thought this was gonna be different."

"If I could make it different, baby, I would. I just need a little understanding from you."

"Is the show more important than me?" I asked. It was a hard question, but I really wanted to know.

My mom's feelings seemed hurt, but mine were all messed up too. We were both silent for a bit. I was so disappointed.

"All I can do, Alec, is pray that you'll understand. It's not more important than you, but it is my job. It's helping to provide a much better life for you. I'll be there soon, just not today. I pray you'll forgive me."

"Whatever," I said under my breath, not wanting to be disrespectful, but just letting out my honest feelings.

This was hard. She told me that she cared, but it felt like she didn't. Her actions were speaking louder than her words. I put down the phone, locked my door, jumped on my bed, and put my face in the pillow.

● ● ●

Sitting in class, I couldn't help but wonder what was going on inside of me. I was looking at Morgan and she looked really pretty. But something else was bothering me too. It was the fact that Morgan and Zarick were standing by the pencil sharpener. They were smiling at each other, but I couldn't hear what they were talking about. I just didn't like the way that she was smiling at him.

I scrambled around in my desk, looking for a pencil. I found two, but both of them had points. So I pushed down hard on my paper and broke them. Why was I doing this? I had no clue, but I had to get over to where they were standing and find out what was going on.

Morgan, a friend of mine, talking to Zarick just didn't sit well with me. I made my way over and stood behind them. Neither one was using the sharpener. They were just laughing together.

Zarick took his finger and played with Morgan's hair. I have to admit that it looked so soft. "Morgan, you look so pretty. I think you could be a model or something," he was telling her.

I had to do something, so I pretended to cough. They both turned around and looked at me.

"Are you gonna sharpen your pencils, or what?" I said, as if they were in my way.

Turning back to face each other, they smiled again. Then Morgan sharpened hers. Zarick rolled his eyes at me and I just stood there, staring at him. He knew that Morgan was my friend, and he could tell that I didn't like the way he was trying to buddy up to her.

Later at lunch, when she was passing by with her tray, Zarick called out, "Hey, Morgan, why don't you sit over here by me?"

Morgan let out a silly laugh and acted all giddy again. I have to admit that I was a little irritated as I watched her put her tray down and sit next to him. Now, I know I didn't ask her to sit by me, but she definitely didn't need to sit by him. This was awful. Zarick was looking at her like he was really interested. All I could do was keep my eyes on them. I didn't even want to eat.

A few minutes later, Trey came and sat down beside me. It didn't take him long to notice that I didn't want to talk to him. The next thing I knew, he was laughing at me.

"Alec, you need to talk to her. If you don't, you're gonna pop from being mad about it."

I hurried to respond. "I'm not mad."

"Somethin' is makin' you boil, and I bet I know what it is. Man, you like her!"

"What are you talkin' about? I do not."

"Then, why are you sittin' here lookin' like the other team just scored a touchdown every time you look over there at Morgan and Zarick?"

I shook my head and denied it again.

"Okay, then, I'm gonna go and tell her that you want to talk to her."

"It doesn't matter what you tell her. I'm gonna deny it, because I don't."

"Okay, cool. I won't say anything to her . . . if you tell me the truth." Trey said, as he slowly started to get up from the lunch table. He was actually calling my bluff.

As soon as he took three steps, I jumped up and pulled him back over to our table.

"Okay, okay, okay. Maybe I do like her," I finally admitted.

"I knew it! Man, you've liked her since the second or third grade. But you've been pushin' her away. Now that she's talkin' to somebody else who's givin' her some attention, you don't like it," Trey said with a lot of confidence.

"Shhh!" I said, as I put my hand over his mouth. "I can't believe you're being so loud! Morgan is lookin' over here. I don't want anybody else to know. Trey, we're supposed to be boys. You've gotta keep this between us. Okay?"

"I got you, man. I got you." Trey said, trying to be real cool. "But it's nothin' to be ashamed of, dude. You like a girl. What's the big deal?"

Still, I wasn't convinced that he would keep my secret. I looked him in the eye because I wanted to make sure he understood. This was personal. After we gave each other a fist bump, I felt like Trey would keep this to himself.

When it was time for our class to leave the lunchroom, I was feeling pretty awful and dragging behind. My dad noticed and came over to me.

"Son, what's going on? Why is your head hanging so low? It looks like you just lost your best friend or something," he said to me.

I didn't know where to go with his questions. I was still watching them, as they walked along in line. Morgan and Zarick weren't holding hands or anything, but the way she kept playfully punching his shoulder, they might as well have been.

"Can I talk to you for a second, Dad?" I asked, unable to take it any longer.

"Sure, let me tell your teacher. I'll give you a pass to class. Meet me in my office."

I did what he told me and a few minutes later, Dad came in. "What's going on, son? Talk to me," he said.

"Promise me you won't get mad?" I said to him, as he nodded. "I'm not sayin' that I lost my best friend, but things are different with Morgan and me. And I'm not happy about it."

"What do you mean, things are different?"

"She's not talkin' to me. She's not playin' with me. She doesn't wanna eat with me. She doesn't wanna hang out," I said, dropping my head low.

"Okay, son, why is that?"

"Well, lately she's been talkin' to that guy named Zarick. Dad, he's not even the kind of boy Morgan should be hangin' out with."

"Why'd you think I'd get mad about this? Are you telling me that you think you like a girl?"

"No. I mean, yes," I said, scratching my head and looking away from him.

"I don't know, Dad. It just feels weird and I really don't like feeling this way. I'm used to not caring about what Morgan does, or anybody else in our class, for that matter. But all day long the only thing I could focus on was her."

"Well, what do you know? My son is growing up. There's nothing wrong with liking a girl, Alec, but let me be clear. You are in the fifth grade and you have to get your feelings under control. Having a girlfriend is out of the question. I don't even allow your brother to have one, and he's in the seventh grade. But I realize that you are growing up. You're changing, and you're going to experience lots of different emotions. Just know that it's okay as long as you pray about them and ask God to help you. You also have to understand that you want the best for your friends. That includes allowing them to grow and not just be around you. There's no need for you to be jealous, son. Nor do you want to keep your feelings hidden."

"So I should tell her?"

"Not right now. I don't think you know exactly what you're feeling. The sooner you involve God and honestly tell Him how you feel, the better. Let me pray for you now," Dad said, as he held out his hand.

I took it and bowed my head.

Then Dad prayed, "Heavenly Father, I thank You for my son, Alec. He's growing up, Lord, but I know if he keeps You at the center of his heart, all these different emotions and feelings he's going through will find their right place. Guide him, Lord. Help him to make wise choices. Help him to keep an open heart toward You and others, not a closed one. In Jesus' name, we do pray. Amen."

I squeezed my dad's hand real tight. Then he gave me a pass, and I walked out of his office with my head held high. For the moment, I felt a little more comfortable, knowing that I could share with my father and trust him with a deep secret.

Letter to Mom

Dear Mom,

Finally, I had to admit it. I confided in Dad that I think my friend Morgan is really special. Dad said that I shouldn't tell her right now, but I should pray and ask God to give me guidance. I hope you don't mind that another girl is important to me. But don't worry, Mom, you'll always be my best girl.

I want to learn karate to defend myself from this bully at school. It's not that I like fighting, but I have to protect myself. I have been petrified of this guy named Zarick, so I really think learning karate is important. Dad is irritated about the whole thing, but I hope you understand, Mom. Can you help me convince Dad that I need to learn self-defense skills right away?

Your son,
Needing your help, Alec

WINNING THE BATTLE

Word Search:

KIHON WAZA (key-hone wah-zah)
BASIC TECHNIQUE

```
U  I  U  M  B  U  T  N  G  I  E  C
T  D  A  O  L  S  C  T  T  L  K  H
B  J  J  R  E  K  U  I  H  C  U  O
N  P  D  O  A  D  I  P  U  I  I  U
Y  N  O  A  N  B  R  P  I  Q  E  I
A  T  U  S  U  O  N  J  I  C  T  Z
K  I  Z  H  W  S  E  A  N  B  O  B
U  V  A  I  T  Q  B  M  D  G  H  V
Z  J  O  D  A  N  U  K  E  E  S  T
U  V  A  A  D  C  E  G  F  B  G  B
K  I  H  C  A  D  N  A  S  I  E  S
I  I  T  H  F  L  X  A  R  M  X  H
```

Gedan Barai (geh-dahn bah-rye): downward block
Jodan Uke (jo-dahn oo-key): upward block
Moro Ashi Dach (moor-oh aah-she dah-chee): fighting stance
Seisan Dachi (say-san dah-chee): forward stance
Shotei Uke (sho-tye oo-key): palm/heel block
Uchi Uke (oo-chee oo-key): inward block
Yaku Zuki (ya-koo zoo-key): reverse punch

Right
Track

3

A week had gone by and so many things were still bothering me. It's no fun getting up extra early to ride to school with my dad. I wasn't thrilled to stand at my safety patrol post either. Besides that, Mom still hadn't come home for a visit. And on top of all that, Zarick and Morgan were hanging out more and more. I hadn't figured out yet how to deal with that situation.

Since I didn't have the best attitude, no one wanted to be around me. Early in the day, I snapped at the teacher a couple of times when she called on me. So now she wasn't trying to make sure I understood the lesson. And honestly, I just wasn't interested in my studies like I used to be.

I mean, who could blame me for being super frustrated? California had my mom, the school had my dad, and Zarick had the girl who's been my friend for a long time.

All of these things kept me up at night because I was feeling like the biggest loser. Dad had me on punishment.

He took away football practice and that was really getting to me. He said it was because my attitude was all wrong. And until I learned to be respectful, I couldn't play.

I tossed and turned and couldn't sleep. I punched the pillows, kicked off the covers, and pulled them back on— over and over again. I tried to count sheep, and that didn't work either. It was a miserable night.

So the next day when Dr. Richardson was going over our math problems, I wasn't listening. I'd been fighting to stay awake, but I guess my body won. Right there in class, I fell asleep. The next thing I knew, there was a loud noise and my dad was standing in front of me. He'd taken my math book and slammed it on the desk to wake me.

"Son! Wake up!" he shouted.

I jumped and the class started laughing. It was so embarrassing.

Immediately, I prayed silently, *"Lord, what's happening to me? I want to do right, but everything seems to be going wrong. School used to come easy to me, but it seems like I've lost interest in it. I'm not a wimp, but I need karate lessons to make me stronger. I really want to try and impress Morgan, but this doesn't look good at all. My dad just yelled at me in front of the whole class. Now everyone is laughing at me like I'm a clown. What am I supposed to do?"*

"Alec! Didn't you hear me? Get up and come with me right now!" my father demanded, not letting up on me.

"Yeah. Go tighten him up, Dr. London," Tyrod said to my dad, as he made a fist and pointed it toward me.

"Tyrod, get to your work!" Dad said to him, "Unless you want to be next." My father wasn't playing when he asked Tyrod, "Is that what you want?"

When Dad gave him a serious stare, Tyrod looked away. He wasn't laughing or trying to be so smart then.

"I didn't think so. Hurry up, Alec!" Dad said, as I walked slowly toward the door.

When we got out into the hallway, he closed the classroom door.

"Yes, Dad?" I asked in a voice that sounded like I didn't want to be bothered.

"What is going on with you, Alec London? This isn't you. You went to bed early last night and now you can't even keep your head up in the classroom. What were you doing all last night that you can't stay awake in school? Where is your iPod?"

"It's at home, Dad, you said I couldn't bring it to school."

"Great. As soon as we get home, I want you to bring it to my room, along with all your video games. This is just ridiculous, son. You know that I want you to set a high example at this school. We've talked about it often enough. Now, how do you think this makes me look?"

"Dad, I'm sorry."

Actually, I wanted to say, *It's not all about you and how I make you look. I have some things going on in my life too.* But I kept my mouth closed because this wasn't the time to press my father too hard.

Instead, I said, "Take everything I have, Dad. I don't deserve to keep anything. I'm a loser." I dropped my head and slumped against the wall.

"Alec, what are you talking about? Do you hear what you're saying?"

"It's always something with me, isn't it? Things never seem to go right . . . I let you down again."

"Son, I didn't say you were a loser. You can win at whatever you want to, so you need to get that idea out of your mind right now. On the other hand, I'm not going to let you trick me into feeling sorry for you either. My job is to be your dad and the principal of this school. That means I will get on you whenever I need to. Sleeping in class is unacceptable. There's nothing wrong with me demanding you to straighten up. So go on back to class and learn something. You're frustrating me because I know you can do better."

Then, seconds later, he softened up a little. When I turned around to leave, Dad placed his hand on my back and said, "Remember, Alec, 'as a man thinks in his heart, so is he.' That's what Proverbs 23:7 says, and I've always told you that."

"But, what does that mean? If I believe in my heart that I can do something, I can do it?" I asked, really unsure.

"That's right, Alec." He gave me a smile and a cheerful look like he was telling me to go on and be great.

I walked back to the classroom, thinking about what Dad just told me. As I passed Tyrod's desk, this time I spotted his foot sticking out, ready to trip me. I wanted to kick it out of my way, but I just stepped over it.

"Your dad obviously didn't knock all the sense out of you," he said, disappointed that I didn't fall for his trick.

I quickly shot back at him, "You sure don't have any. You want me to knock some into you? Step to me, step to me."

Tyrod stood up. We were face-to-face with each other when Dr. Richardson rushed over and ordered, "Tyrod, sit down and keep your mouth shut before I take Dr. London up on his offer and send you to the office. Do not try me, young man; sit down!"

Sounding like a scared little girl, Tyrod squealed, "He started it!"

"Well, I'm ending it," she replied. "Alec, you go and sit down too." Dr. Richardson had the toughest look I'd seen so far on her face.

She wasn't the only one who was angry. My face showed how angry I was too. My eyes were squinted, my lips were poked out, and it felt like steam was coming out of my ears. I was so fed up.

The teacher knew I was upset and told me, "Calm down. Acting this way is not going to solve any problems." As if that wasn't enough, she leaned over, looked me in the eye, and said, "Do you understand?" I didn't answer, and she asked me again, "Alec, do you understand?"

"Yes, ma'am," I finally responded.

"So then, let the hot air out of that balloon and chill."

I heard what she said. I heard my dad. I knew what I was supposed to do, but I still couldn't change the way I felt. At that point, I didn't know what could make things right.

● ● ●

"Alec, I know you're trying to be a loner right now, but I figure I need to tell you something."

"What is it, Trey?" I said, not really interested in whatever he had to say.

"The word is out that Zarick and Tyrod are gonna jump you during recess."

I couldn't act like I didn't care at that point because, by now, everybody knew Zarick was fierce when it came to fighting. My insides started squirming like there were worms crawling around in there. What was I going to do?

"You want me to tell your dad? Maybe you should stay inside for extra tutoring. You want me to jump in and help, or what? I just can't let you go down like that. I can't have you walk into a trap." Trey's face looked serious, as he waited for me to respond.

I'd been treating my best buddy wrong by staying to myself, but there's been so much stuff for me to deal with these days. Yet, none of it was about him. As much as I tried to push Trey away, he still kept coming back to look out for me.

So instead of turning him away this time, I put my hand on his shoulder and said, "Look, thanks for caring. I appreciate you, Trey, but I'm going to handle this my own way."

Challenging me, he shot back, "All right, all right, what way is that?" Trey stood waiting patiently for my answer. When I said nothing, he stepped in to make sure I knew this was a big deal. "We know Tyrod is all talk and no action, but Zarick? Come on, he's another story."

Just then, Dr. Richardson spoke up. "No talking back there. Let's begin the lesson on similes." As she started writing on the board, she explained, "A simile is a figure of speech that compares two things that are not alike. Similes are introduced by the words, 'like' or 'as.' For example, take the sentence: *The twelve- year-old boy cried like a baby.* The simile is: *like a baby.* Now, what can we conclude from that sentence?"

Morgan raised her hand, and Dr. Richardson called on her. "Yes, Morgan."

"A twelve-year-old boy doesn't usually cry really hard, but in this case, the kid was sad, crying out of control. You know, like babies do when they want something."

Dr. Richardson responded, "Exactly. Next sentence: *She was moving as slow as molasses.* The simile there is: *as molasses.* Can anybody tell me what the sentence means?"

"What's molasses?" Tyrod blurted out.

"Duh, it's a type of syrup," Trey answered him.

"Good, Trey, but be respectful. Now, can you tell me more about the sentence?" asked Dr. Richardson.

"Yes, ma'am. When you pour molasses, it doesn't run

fast like water does. It's pretty thick, so it takes its time and goes really slow. So when you compare it to how the girl was running, it means she wasn't going fast."

Dr. Richardson said, "Very good. Now, class, I'm going to name a few more examples. I want you to give me a simile that completes each sentence. Number one, *He was as happy ___.*"

Zarick raised his hand and said, *"as Tyrod, the clown."*

Everyone started laughing except two people—Tyrod and me. That's because I didn't care, and Tyrod was mad.

Our teacher said, "All right. Let's not use any real names in the examples, but that was a good simile."

"So you're sayin' I'm a clown, Dr. Richardson?"

"No, Tyrod. I can see how someone would compare a happy person to a clown because clowns are always happy. Let's not get sensitive. Particularly, when we want to be thought of as tough, right?

Tyrod straightened back up and replied, "Yeah, I'm tough. I'm just sayin'. . ." Then, of course, he said nothing.

"Okay, Tyrod, you give me the next one," said Dr. Richardson. *"The girl was as hungry as ___."*

"The girl was as hungry as a cat," Tyrod shouted out with confidence.

"Tyrod, are cats known to be hungry?" asked Dr. Richardson.

"Well, the stray that keeps comin' into my yard every day is."

"Okay, then that's a good one. However, keep in mind

when you make a simile, most of the time you want to use something that is not related to just one specific example. They should be compared to something that animals and objects are generally known for. For instance: *Her stare was as cold as ice.* The simile is understood because everyone knows that ice is cold. You wouldn't say someone's stare is as cold as a banana because bananas aren't usually cold."

After finishing her explanation, Dr. Richardson said, "Now, class, finish the rest of the problems on your sheet, and then you can go out for recess."

Fifteen minutes later, we were on the blacktop. Kids were splitting up into their usual groups. Most of the boys started playing a game of dodge ball. The girls wasted no time in picking up their jump rope competition. I have to admit, they were pretty awesome.

Thinking about the lesson we just finished, I decided I wasn't going to be a scared little mouse. There's no way Tyrod and Zarick were going to get the best of me. *Alec is as tough as the Incredible Hulk,* I told myself.

When recess time was almost over, I walked over to the swings. Tyrod and Zarick hadn't said a word to me. They were in another area playing soccer with the kickball. Just when I thought there wasn't going to be any problem, the red ball they were playing with rolled over toward me. The two of them rushed up to get it.

"You mean, you can't even hand us the ball?" said Tyrod.

"Yeah, dude. You see the ball is right there. Bend down

and pick it up," Zarick said in a mean tone.

The two of them stepped closer to me, but I wasn't going to run. I wasn't going to scream. I wasn't going to cry. I just stood up from the swing and looked at both of them, daring Zarick to hit me with his magical karate moves. I was scared, but I wasn't going to let them know.

Then Zarick said something I really didn't want to hear. "I see you over there lookin' when Morgan is talkin' to me. She's a cutie. She likes me. Ha ha . . . now, what you gonna do about it?"

"If you're right, she has bad taste. But, that's her decision . . . nothin' I care to do about it."

"Please. I know you're jealous. She likes my moves. Do I need to use them on you? Do I need to make you get down there and give me that ball?"

Tired of being pushed around, I said, "I'm not givin' you the ball. If you want it, then get down there and get it yourself."

"Aww, he's talkin' bad, Tyrod. He disrespects me just like you said. Man, I need to show him a little somethin' somethin'."

Just as soon as Zarick raised his hands, Morgan yelled out, "Zarick, what are you doin'? I know you're not gonna hit Alec. I thought we talked about that. You said you weren't gonna be doin' that to people anymore."

"He's the one who started somethin' with me," he shot back.

Morgan rushed up to us. "Come on, Zarick. I heard

everything you said. Leave Alec alone. He can't defend himself against you."

Tyrod and Zarick gave each other a fist bump and started laughing real loud.

"She said it, man. Alec can't handle you," Tyrod said it like it was a big joke. He looked over at me, grabbed the ball, and dashed away with Zarick.

Morgan came closer and asked me, "Are you okay?"

I couldn't say anything and darted toward the school door. I was so upset. I didn't need her to help me. I didn't want her to interfere, and she didn't need to think that I couldn't defend myself against bullies. Even if I couldn't, her help was the last person's help I wanted. I was going to have to do something about this. Quick!

● ● ●

"Alec, honey, you've been cramped up in this here old room of yours for too long. You need to come on with me to my church revival," said Grandma, as she poked her head into my room.

It hadn't been that long since I had given my life to the Lord. To be honest, I was a little salty at God because, try as I might to be a very good person, things weren't going my way. That was really stressing me. But, the more I thought about it, maybe she had a good idea. Maybe going to church would help. She was right. I'd been cooped up in my room all weekend. Couldn't go to football practice, couldn't do karate, and didn't want to ride my bike outside with Morgan. So maybe going to church was a good thing.

"Yes, ma'am. I'll go."

"Oh, good! Well, get on up. I can't be late now. We'll be leaving out of here in twenty minutes."

As soon as she walked away, I got down on my knees and prayed. *"Lord, I'm sorry for questioning You. I know that You know what's best. I believe You love me, and I know You sent Your Son to die on the cross for my sins. I just didn't think it would be this hard to be a Christian. Please help me because I'm tired of being stuck in this rut. In Jesus' name, I pray. Amen."*

God heard my prayer because the service was off the chain. The choir was jamming. I was on my feet clapping and feeling the beat, wishing I could be on the drums throwing down. One guy did a praise dance, and everyone seemed to feel the Spirit of God moving through the church—including me.

Then, there was a cool skit where the main character was having all kinds of trouble until he asked God to help him. All the way to the end, the Lord was working to help the guy out. Sitting there watching it play out, I could only hope the same thing would happen for me. I kept thinking how much I wanted God to hear my prayer and make my life better.

By the time the guest minister came to the pulpit and announced, "The title of my sermon today is, 'I Hear You Calling Me, and I'm Listening,'" I was ready.

A lady behind me said, "Amen!"

I wanted to say "Amen" too. No one knows what other people in the congregation are going through, but as I looked around, people had tears in their eyes before he even said a word. It seems like the praise and worship time had already made a difference. I was just a kid sitting there, so I couldn't even pretend to imagine adult problems. But I do know that it's a good thing that there is a place we can all come to for help when we need it.

So I listened as the minister said, "I just dropped by this evening, not to take too much of your time, but just to let you know that God hears, and He cares. I'll say it again, God hears, and He cares. No matter what's going on in your life, there is no problem too big for God. You see, sometimes we get too caught up in our own problems and the things that we're going through. We forget about the only One who can truly make a difference. But, once we go to Jesus and tell Him about our struggles and our woes, we have to be still and let Him work things out."

Wow, I thought, as I listened to every word he was saying. I couldn't wait to hear more. The minister went on to say, "You see, we think that we've got to do something to fix it. But it's when you turn your troubles over to Jesus and leave them there, when you trust Him, that you can rest. Relax, trust, have faith, and stand. The Word says, in Psalm 46:10, to, *'be still and know that I am God.'* It doesn't say give it to God and keep on fretting. You have to know that He can handle it and believe it. You have to know that He wants you to keep your focus on Him and not on your problems. When you learn to depend on the Lord and stay focused on His goodness and not on your troubles, if you let Him into your heart and allow Him take over your circumstances, then you've got all you need. So remember, no more crying and worrying—just rejoice in God. Be still and know that He can do it!"

People all around me rose to their feet. The choir started singing and I was smiling. The minister didn't say when God would fix things; he only said God would fix them. When we were leaving out, I looked around and was surprised to see the karate instructor in the crowd.

I went right up to him and said, "Oh, Mr. Stone! I'm ready now. You've gotta train me. Please."

"Slow down, Alec. It's good to see you. You really are excited. Why do you think you're ready for karate now?"

"Well, because this girl . . . and she . . ."

"Wait, wait, now you want to learn it because of a girl?"

I couldn't believe I said that.

"Son, you're still not ready."

He walked away. I was so angry and frustrated with myself. Somehow, I had to get on the right track.

Letter to Mom

Dear Mom,

What a frustrating day I've had. I tried to impress Morgan, but instead only embarrassed myself. Mom, being laughed at is totally unacceptable for me. Tyrod and Zarick are still trying to push me around. I am so tired of it.

I hope you understand from my letters how upset I am. I have been praying, and I was thankful Grandma took me to her church revival. What the minister said is really helping me work through my problems. The service was great, and it seemed like the entire congregation enjoyed it. I'll keep praying.

　　　　Your son,

　　　　Standing on faith, Alec

Word Search:

TE WAZA (tay wah-zah)
HAND TECHNIQUES, Part 1

```
O  V  H  M  P  V  M  R  D  D  S  P
V  D  D  I  N  Q  F  R  U  H  S  Q
M  P  B  G  J  C  S  I  C  D  S  E
X  I  K  S  V  I  H  I  Q  R  K  O
F  J  D  Y  J  C  A  B  A  H  Y  Z
A  G  E  Z  U  K  E  T  I  A  S  L
K  I  O  I  Q  H  T  K  E  I  H  T
C  U  P  B  A  O  E  V  N  S  L  G
B  M  E  R  J  T  T  M  V  H  E  S
E  J  R  G  E  T  P  I  F  U  H  C
S  W  O  T  U  K  A  K  A  U  P  I
T  B  Y  U  Y  Z  G  D  N  H  V  B
```

Age Zuke (ah-geh zoo-key): rising punch
Empi Uchi (em-pee oo-chee): elbow strike
Haishu (hi-shoo): back of hand
Haito (hi-toe): knife hand
Hiji Ate (he-gee ah-tay): elbow smash
Hike Te (hee-key tay): withdrawing hand; the hand on the hip
Kakuto (kah-koo-toe): bent wrist

62

not
Fair

4

"Something is wrong with this! You mean, I have a C in English, a C in Social Studies, a C in Math, and a C in Science? Dr. Richardson, this can't be right," I said, with a big attitude. She had just called me up to her desk and given me my progress report.

Walking back to my seat, I had to admit to myself that I hadn't gotten the best grades lately. However, I didn't think I did bad enough to get Cs in everything! I couldn't stop shaking my head in disbelief. Somehow it didn't seem fair. I wanted my teacher to take out her calculator and figure up my averages again.

"Alec London, come here," she said, as she motioned with her finger for me to come back to her desk. "Do not shout across my room! If you need to speak to me or ask me a question, be respectful and come up here to do so. Your grades are your grades. They are what they are. If you don't like them, then do better. I am not going to give you a grade you didn't earn."

"But you told me that I was going to get a chance to do some stuff over again. I remember seeing a couple of tests scores where my grade was below fifty, but it was only one or two," I responded.

"Okay, well, you take a score below fifty; which, by the way, was a fifteen on your math quiz. Add that to another exam grade that was a seventy-nine. Divide that by two because you've only had two tests so far and that equals an F. Because you've done some homework, not all, some class work, not all, it brought your grade up from an F to a C. And even with that I'm being more than fair. So drop the attitude with me, young man. If you're going to be mad at anyone—be mad at yourself."

Mumbling to myself, I replied, "You're the teacher. It's your fault if my grades are like this."

"Who are you talking to?" my upset teacher said with a stern voice.

Tyrod jumped up out of his seat and said, "Oooooo! Let him have it, Doc!"

"Sit down, Tyrod! I don't need any help from you. I've got this," Dr. Richardson said in her very cool slang voice.

Ignoring our teacher, Tyrod yelled out to me, "Oooooo, you're gonna be in trouble when you get home. Your daddy's gonna tear you up!"

I rushed over to him, and he met me half way. We were standing chest to chest, ready to take each other on. Everyone knows we're not friends, and that's just the way it is.

Dr. Richardson quickly came over and made us back

away from each other. "Tyrod, go and sit down! Alec, you need to go to the washroom and calm down! Don't come back in here with all that frustration and anger."

"Whatever!" I said, extremely upset.

Minutes later, I was in the washroom splashing some cool water on my face. Not knowing what else to do, I put my head against the wall and prayed, *"Lord, I don't know why I'm so angry. I don't know why I'm so upset. I don't know why I'm so mad. I just am. I want to have a better attitude and be happy. The side of me that wants to be upset is winning. I'm not focused. I'm losing my friends, and I just need You to help me."*

Later on, when I got home and Dad saw my progress report, it felt like the Lord hadn't heard me at all. There was no mercy and no grace. I got no help in keeping me from my dad's anger

"Do you know why I'm so disappointed in you, Alec?" he asked me. "Your number one job is to go to school, learn your lessons, and give one-hundred percent so you can succeed. Cs, Alec? Come on, man. You aren't even trying. Do you know you were on track to be a doctor?"

Shaking my head and frowning, I let out a sigh and told him, "I never said I want to be a doctor."

"Don't get smart with me, boy. I didn't say that you did. I'm trying to tell you that it's the kind of potential you have. But you aren't giving that type of effort. In the end, you're only hurting yourself. And believe me, you're going to regret it. You are my son and I know that you're capable of high achievement. I'm not going to tolerate you being below average. "

"But Dad, it's been really hard lately, I said.

My father wasn't going to accept any excuses. He stuck to his point and laid down the law, "I want you to do your best, son. Right now, you're not doing all you can. If I have to, I'll examine every piece of homework that goes out of this house. I'll make sure I know when you have a test and quiz you beforehand. From now on, that's how we're going to handle it."

"You're okay if Antoine makes Cs," I responded, trying to get some relief.

"You're not Antoine. Besides, just like I'm pushing you, I'm pushing him too. He's not going to get away with any-thing—and neither are you. In this house, I'm the father. Now, what else do you have to show me?"

"It's just some little note. You don't have to read it . . . just sign it right there."

"Boy, do I look like I was born yesterday? Did you forget that I am the principal of the school? I saw Dr. Richardson today, and she told me I wouldn't be too happy. I thought she was just talking about your grades, but a letter too?" He took a minute to read it and then snarled at me like a grizzly bear does when he's grumpy. "She's saying you were disrespectful to her in class! Alec, what is wrong with you?"

I couldn't explain it to him because I couldn't explain it to myself. Something was wrong with me, but I didn't know what it was. I just wasn't happy with me, and I was tired of people pushing me around. I was also tired of being "nice Alec." It seems like I get more respect when I just call things like I see them.

I huffed and said, "I think teachers are responsible for grades. I made all Cs, and you think I should have better grades than what I have. That's Dr. Richardson's fault. She told me my poor grades weren't going to stick, but there they are."

"What? Don't blame her for your problems. You need to take responsibility for your own actions. Don't worry, though. I'm going to help you get it right, son. You can count on that. Go to your room, get your books, and study for one hour in every one of them. Then, I want you to write Dr. Richardson an apology letter. The next time you act smart with a teacher, I'll have no problem giving you a punishment you won't soon forget. In fact, until further notice, you'll be responsible for cleaning this entire house—from top to bottom. Understand?"

I just looked at him and couldn't believe what I was hearing.

"Do you understand?"

"Yes, sir," I quickly responded, hoping my father didn't intend to enforce this horrible punishment.

● ● ●

"Okay, first, you need to clean my gym shoes, vacuum my carpet, make my bed, paint my walls, and . . . "

"Wait, wait, what are you talkin' about?" I said to Antoine, as he rattled off a list of crazy things I was supposed to do for him.

"Dad said you need to help me clean up my stuff."

"Yeah, *help* is the key word. No way I'm touchin' your shoes."

"I was just playin'. But, for real, Alec, it does mean you've gotta clean up my bedroom."

"I'm not your maid. I'm gonna have to talk to Dad about this. He couldn't intend for me to clean your room," I said to him.

Antoine replied, "Well, I did hear him say the whole house, from top to bottom. But don't worry, little dude, you're off the hook. I don't want you messin' around in my room anyway."

Grandma had been resting more lately. Since she wasn't up and about as much, work around the house was undone. And because I was in trouble with my grades, my dad was making me do all the housework. He gave me orders to take out the trash, wash the breakfast and dinner dishes, wash my clothes, wash, fold, and put away the towels, and rake the falling leaves. Basically, I'm responsible for everything!

After I straightened up the family room, Antoine came behind me with a bag of cookies and turned on the TV. He flopped down on the sofa and started dropping crumbs all over the floor. When I vacuumed the carpet a second time, he just sat there watching me. I knew he was thinking, *Uh huh, yeah. I'm lovin' this.*

Antoine thought this was funny and I was boiling mad. It felt like torture. He told me it was about time that I was the one cleaning up and being on punishment. I kept thinking to myself, *I never want to be in the position of letting Dad down again.*

Seeing him chilling out made me want to go to Dad and vent, but I knew I didn't have a leg to stand on. I hadn't done my part in school, and I had to suffer the consequences. I could hear Dad saying, *If you don't like it, do what you're supposed to do. Then you won't have to go through this again.*

I was just about finished cleaning our bathroom. The only thing left to do was wash out the bathtub. That yucky chore gave me a newfound appreciation for the fact that Grandma gets down on her knees to scrub it. The nasty, dark brown ring around the tub was disgusting. Man, we boys sure know how to dirty things up. I promised myself to rinse it out after every bath from now on.

The cleaning product reeked with strong chemicals, and I could hardly stand it. Antoine stood in the doorway and started coughing. I turned around because I thought he was just making fun of me again.

"Oh, okay. Go ahead. Let it out . . . laugh," I said to him.

"Naw, bro. I came in here to encourage you and see if you need help."

I almost passed out. I couldn't believe he really wanted to help me. He didn't have to. Antoine wasn't in trouble.

What was this all about? Not saying a word, I just looked up at him, waiting for whatever was coming next.

"Okay, all right, I really don't wanna help you. But, I do want to talk to you."

I turned back around and started scrubbing harder. "Go ahead."

Antoine's words turned serious. "Wassup with you, man? Dad's right. You've got so much potential, Alec. I can see it. Dad pushes me too, but he doesn't expect as much out of me."

"That's not true."

"Okay, he expects a lot out of both of us, but he really expects a lot from you. You pick up stuff real easy. You used to like learnin' and bein' challenged. For most kids, if the teacher isn't teachin' anything, we don't care. But not you, Alec. You used to demand your education. You wanna learn stuff. You wanna be smart. It's cool. Don't change that. Is anybody pickin' on you, or whatever, just because you make good grades? Is that why you don't wanna be smart anymore? Is that what's goin' on?"

I shrugged my shoulders and honestly wished that was the reason. Any reason was better than no reason at all.

"You don't have to talk to me, but I think you're sellin' yourself short. I just want you to know that I'm here, if you need me. That's all."

I got off of my knees and turned the water on to rinse out the tub. Then I gave Antoine a grin big enough to let him know I appreciated him talking to me. Hoping my work was complete for the day, I put the sponge in the bucket and carried it down to the kitchen sink. Dad was sitting at the table, eating a sandwich.

"Is there anything else, sir? I'm finished."

"No, I know you've done a lot of cleaning since you got home. Your grandmother will appreciate it. Now, I want you to go to your room and put on that karate suit that's been hanging up for a while. I'm going to take you in for a lesson," he said with a slight smile.

He just didn't know how happy I was to hear those words. Hurrying up the stairs, I got more and more excited! Mr. Stone must have told my dad that he was ready to teach me. As I put on my uniform, I could see myself kicking that bag and learning all the cool moves.

As soon as Dad dropped me off, Mr. Stone greeted me. He was being very nice and asked me how I'd been. Then he asked if I was finally ready to do karate for the right reasons.

Just when I thought we were going to get started, he took me into his office and put some cleaning tools in my hands. I was confused. The man who was supposed to be teaching me karate skills told me to clean his floor.

"Now, I don't want you to do it just any old way. I want you to take off the old polish this way and then rub some more on that way." He showed me the movements as he explained. "I want it done right. I don't want to see any black marks. You got it?"

I just stood there, looking at him like he was joking. I'd

been cleaning like crazy at home. The last thing I wanted to do was come to his gym wearing my cool white karate outfit, ready to learn, and then have to get on my knees and clean some more.

When I didn't move, he turned around and said, "Do I need to call your dad and tell him you're not ready to learn what I have to teach you?"

I didn't know if he was threatening me or trying to scare me. It took so long to get back here that the last thing I wanted to do was make him mad. He might want to kick me out again.

Over the last week and a half, I had become a good housekeeper. I looked down at the floor in his small office. My session was an hour and a half. I was wondering how long it would take me to get the job done. Hopefully, he would still have time to teach me some karate moves.

After thirty minutes passed, Mr. Stone came and inspected my work. Then, he directed me to the dressing room. Pointing to the floor, he told me, "Clean this one the same way." His orders were really starting to get to me, and I guess it showed on my face. The next thing my karate teacher said was, "What's wrong, son? Why are your lips poking out like you don't want to do this? You saw the movie *Karate Kid*. Right? Well, just like in that story, everything I do has a purpose."

"It was a long time ago, and I guess I fell asleep on some parts. I don't remember it all," I explained.

Mr. Stone responded, "Trust me. I've been doing this

for a long time, Alec. You have to be open to learn."

"It just doesn't seem like I'm learnin' anything," I complained.

"You just get to it."

That's all he said before he walked away. The other kids were out on the floor learning some cool karate moves. But I had to continue scrubbing the floor, taking old polish off and rubbing more on. I wasn't even sure if I wanted to come back again because—regardless of what he said—this just didn't seem right.

● ● ●

"Lord," I prayed silently. *"I'm just coming to You now because I'm really worried about Grandma. She's been complaining of not feeling well, and she hasn't been up and around lately. I don't know what's wrong, but she doesn't want to go to the doctor. Just help her, Lord. Help her to feel better or give her the courage to go and get checked out. She always says she didn't come here to stay. A part of me didn't want her to stay in my home at first, but after she got sick last year and was in the hospital, I realized how much she means to me. I really need her to be with us. I'll even keep cleaning after my punishment is done. Just make her stronger, please. In Jesus' name, I pray. Amen."*

"Well, Andre, if you think I need to go, then I'm gonna go ahead and go to the doctor," Grandma told my father, right after I said my prayer.

Dad's eyes started watering a little, but it was a good

kind of teary eyed. I knew he was concerned about her. He'd been trying hard to convince her to talk to the doctor about the results of the tests she took last month. Dad had been practically waiting on her hand and foot since then. Now, he was elated that his mother had finally given in.

"I guess I'm gonna be okay, lettin' them doctors poke on me again," Grandma said with a smile, as she hugged Antoine and me. Then she complained all the way to the door. "I just don't know what the big deal is about goin' to the doctor. All they do is run a lot of tests and keep you comin' back. Well, I don't need nobody workin' on me and checkin' me out. I'm just gettin' on up there in age, that's all."

"Grandma, some people came to our school and talked about the fact that everyone should get yearly checkups. That way, the doctor can find out when stuff is wrong. Then, he can give you a proper diagnosis," I told her.

"Look at my grandson, using them big old words. Let me go on then. Let 'em diagnosis me."

"I'm sure they just need to give you some medicine, Grandma, and everything's gonna be fine."

"Alec, while we're gone, you can walk on over to Morgan's house," Dad told me. "Her mom said it's okay for you guys to work on your project together."

"Just make sure you're respectful," Grandma added, before Dad shut the door behind them.

"Alec's goin' to his girlfriend's house!" teased Antoine.

I stood there, refusing to let him get to me. I already

had a lot on my mind and pretty much tuned him out. Actually, I was thinking of Morgan and the way I've been treating her lately. Morgan is really cool, but she probably didn't like the fact that Dr. Richardson made us partners on the science fair project.

"You mean, you aren't gonna jump down my throat?" Antoine interrupted my thoughts and said to me. "I'm just teasin' you. Say somethin'."

"It's cool. I'm really worried about Grandma. Remember, last year Dad took her to the hospital and she had to stay. On top of that, I know Morgan is upset with me. Now I've gotta go over to her house. It's like somethin' is always goin' on. I can never just be cool. So I know she doesn't think I'm cool."

Surprisingly, Antoine said something that made a lot of sense. "You ever thought of just bein' honest and tellin' her what's goin' on. I mean, I thought y'all used to talk. I'm in the seventh grade, and I haven't met a girl yet as cool as Morgan. It seems to me like you can tell her anything, and she just tries to help you."

I nodded, because he was right. She is a good friend. So I got my backpack and headed to her house. Besides, it was important for us to work on our science project.

As soon as I got there, Morgan could tell something was up. "What's wrong?" she asked me.

I don't know if she saw it on my face, if I was walking way too slow, or what, but she knew something wasn't right. As always, Morgan wanted to help.

"We can't work on our science project until you have some pep in your step."

"Pep in my step? What does that mean?"

"You know, some get up and go! You've gotta conquer the battle going on inside you, Alec. I told you, it's all about attitude. Whatever's goin' on, if you have a frown on your face, it's gonna feel worse."

"So you think I'm supposed to smile, even when I don't feel like it?" I asked. To me, that made no sense.

"Yes, because it lightens your load. I mean, have you tried it? If you haven't . . . what do you have to lose? Come on," she said, as she started tickling my arm like she had an invisible feather or something. I couldn't stop laughing.

"Wow, thanks," I said, feeling a little better after letting out a big laugh that turned into an even bigger smile. Then I told her, "I was pretty sad because my Grandma is on her way to the doctor. She hasn't been well for a while. The last time she went for a checkup, they ran some tests. Ever since then, she's been scared to go back."

Morgan had just helped me lighten my mood, and I started thinking maybe things would be okay. I was really thankful.

After that, she switched to business. "Okay. Now, we can get to work. Remember our title, 'Are Permanent Markers Really Permanent?' Now what's our hypothesis?"

"Well," I said to her, "Permanent markers aren't really permanent. Think about when you get a mark on your shirt. After you wash it, the mark goes away. So I think our hypothesis should either be: 'permanent markers are not really permanent.' Or, better yet: 'we will prove that permanent markers are not really permanent'."

As she turned on her Mom's laptop, Morgan nodded and said, "Sounds good to me. Let's do some research."

An hour later when I got back home, Dad and Grandma weren't there yet. The way Antoine was pacing around the house, it gave me the impression that everything wasn't okay.

Putting his hands on his head, he quickly blurted out, "Dad called and said he's pickin' up some dinner. But the way he said it, Alec, I don't know. I'm just nervous."

To see how uneasy my brother was acting made me know this was a lot. Antoine was usually cooler than a fan spinning a cool breeze in the summertime. He didn't let anything rattle him.

"We've got to think positive. Everything's gonna be okay," I said to him, learning something from Morgan.

Shooting down my idea, Antoine said, "Don't you understand? If everything was okay, Dad would have just told me that on the phone. I asked him."

"Well, I don't know what you asked him. I wasn't here."

"Okay, well, I'm tellin' you now. I asked Dad if everything was okay, and he said we'll talk about it when he gets home. He was real short and cut me off. Somethin's not right. What we gonna do without Grandma?"

Taking a long sigh, I said, "We can pray."

"I don't wanna pray," Antoine said and stormed away.

He went straight to his room and slammed the door. Ten minutes later, we heard my father's car pull up. Antoine flew back down the stairs, and we both rushed to open the front door.

As soon as we got to the car, Antoine opened the door on Grandma's side. It was a relief to see her, but she said something right away that sounded like trouble. "It's gonna be okay, boys. At least I know why I've had this precious time with y'all."

"What are you sayin', Grandma?" asked Antoine, as he helped her out of her seat.

Standing there in the driveway, she gave us the news, "Baby, I got that cancer. Those tests they ran came back and said so."

Dad hung his head down. I clung to Grandma's chest. Antoine screamed out, "That's not fair!"

Letter to Mom

Dear Mom,

I don't know if God is angry with me or what. Dad said I am not living up to my potential. He thinks I'm not giving enough effort in school. I made all Cs on my progress report and that's not good enough. I know you want me to excel and make all As, and Dad does too.

Then, we got some really bad news. To add to my down days, the doctor said that Grandma has cancer. At first, I was very worried to tell you that, since you are away. But I'm sure Dad already told you. It's just not fair, Mom. Please pray for her.

Your son,

Hoping for a breakthrough, Alec

Word Search:

TE WAZA (tay wah-zah)
HAND TECHNIQUES, Part 2

A	D	C	R	E	A	N	F	R	D	T	U
H	N	D	G	F	T	V	G	D	C	Z	U
V	S	J	G	U	S	I	W	N	O	Z	J
I	U	S	T	T	E	T	K	H	N	A	K
K	L	P	H	M	E	L	S	U	Z	E	Y
U	I	M	P	Z	O	I	U	W	N	C	T
Z	W	X	L	U	E	D	I	T	S	S	L
I	L	M	E	T	V	W	S	N	D	T	F
O	S	N	F	B	P	U	Q	H	O	I	C
J	C	U	O	W	I	K	S	O	U	N	K
U	R	A	K	E	N	A	B	A	C	T	L
A	T	B	D	P	M	G	H	P	C	Q	O

Kentsui (ken-t-sue-ee): hammer fist
Nukite (noo-key-tay): spear hand
Oi Zuki (oh-ee zoo-key): lunge punch
Shuto (shoo-toe): knife hand
Teisho (tay-show) or Shotei (show-tay): palm heel
Tettsui (tay-t-sue-ee): hammer fist
Uraken (ree-kin): back fist

Feel Better

5

I couldn't stop the tears from flowing. It was so upsetting to hear the news that my grandmother had cancer. I didn't know where cancer came from or how people got it, but I knew it was nothing to play with. Why Grandma? It just didn't seem right.

When we got inside the house, I fell into my Grandma's arms again.

"You've gotta be okay, Grandma. I can't lose you," I said softly.

My father just left out of the room. He was all choked up. Antoine opened up the front door and ran down the street. He didn't want to let anybody see him cry. I wanted to be tough, but I couldn't hold in my sadness either.

Grandma said, "Oh, Alec, honey, I'm gon' be okay."

"How are you gonna be okay if you have cancer? I don't understand. This isn't good. What's gonna happen?"

"Well, they're gonna give me a treatment plan, and we're gonna see how it works out. It's not over 'til it's over, baby. And if I have one more day on this Earth or many, many, more, I'm gon' live my time with a happy heart. So if I see tears, they better be tears of joy and not sorrow," she said, wiping my eyes.

Grandma was trying to pull back so she could look down at my face, but I didn't want to let her go. I didn't want to hurt her by squeezing her too tight either, not being sure if she was in any pain.

She was my grandmother, and she'd become so important to me. She'd been here for Dad, Antoine, and me almost every day since last year. Imagining a world without her in it wasn't a thought I could be happy about. So as Grandma tried to pull apart from me, I felt as if I was really losing her. I thought about her being gone, and it made me cry louder and harder, until I almost couldn't breathe.

When Dad heard me, he rushed back into the room. "Son, are you okay? Are you okay?" he kept asking me.

"No! I'm not okay!" I said back.

"Now, my men have gotta relax," Grandma said, as she sat down in a chair.

Just then, we heard the front door close.

"Antoine, come on in here," Grandma called out, as Dad rubbed my back.

"Dad, this is hard. I feel sick myself," I whispered, unable to get ahold of my bad thoughts.

All three of us stood in front of her. Like a drill sergeant, Grandma told us, "Listen up, and I'm only gon' tell y'all this one time. I didn't get the news I wanted today, but

I'm a child of the King, and He knows what's best. We all love Him, and we trust Him. Who knows, but Jesus, what tomorrow holds. We didn't come to this world to stay forever. Andre, son, you know that. And boys, I know you're young, but I'll tell you one thing—when we leave this world we're going to be with the Lord. So I'll be all right with whatever happens next. I'm not in a panic and I don't want y'all to be either." When she finished talking, Grandma held out her arms for all of us to hug her.

"You're right, Mom," Dad said, giving her a big hug. "I have to be an example for these boys. But you're my mom, and you know I care about you."

"I know, son. But there are some things I want to do. Like right now, let's go skating!"

Antoine looked at Grandma real hard and said, "Huh, you wanna skate? You can't skate, Grandma."

"Aww, that's my boy. That's what I'm talkin' about. Go on and show that spunk I love. Oh, and yes, I can. I can probably run circles around you young folks. I can skate backwards, to the side, to the front. I can spin too. Well, I used to a long time ago, anyway."

"She taught me how to skate, boys," Dad said to us. "You sure you're up to it, Mom?"

Grandma said, "This old body of mine is gonna be hurtin' for a while. If I concentrate on havin' fun and not on what ails me, it'll be well worth it. So can we get rid of these long faces and go and have a good time?"

Later at the skating rink, it was amazing to see Antoine

hold our grandmother's hands to help her keep her balance. Once it all came back to her, she was skating on her own. Not that fast, but she wasn't falling down. She was smiling, and that was all that mattered.

Dad and I sat there watching her. "Your Grandma is right, you know," he said to me, as he kept his eyes on his precious mother.

"Right about what?"

"We didn't come into this world to stay. We've got to enjoy every moment."

"God knows the plan," I said, saying what I had been taught. "But sometimes it hurts. Sometimes what we go through seems too tough to me."

"That's when we can't give up. We have to pray and ask God to give us strength when we're weak. And most important, we must keep in mind that the battle isn't ours. It's God's. He can cure my mom. He can help us not be afraid. God can do anything, but fail. He's the best parent in the entire world."

It felt so good to hear Dad's positive words. Then he asked me, "You don't always agree with my decisions, do you?"

I thought to myself, *Oh, Dad, you just don't know how much your decisions make me upset sometimes.* Without saying anything, I gave him a look that said it all. He just smiled, letting me know that he understood.

"Yep, see. I know. But you know I love you, and I want the best for you. Even when I give you tough love it's for your good. While I can't imagine my mom not in my life, and you not having your grandmother, if that's what happens, we have to accept it. As a matter of fact, our heavenly Father will help us accept it. Besides, I know if that were the case, heaven will be richer if she's there."

Confused, I asked, "You think we'll be better if she's gone?"

"What I mean is, we'll be better because we'll know she won't be hurting anymore. We'll be better because she's always been a great mom and grandma. We'll be better because we'll always try to make her proud."

"Dad, I really don't want her to go."

"I know, son. I don't either."

"God is a miracle worker," I said to my father, believing God can heal her.

"Yes, He is," Dad said calmly. "And when two or more agree on something, the Bible says the Lord is in their midst. Let's wait on God and see. We'll keep a smile and have faith in Him."

● ● ●

"There he is right over there, Zarick. That little wimp, Alec, is sittin' all alone. He's got no backup from his other little wimpy friends who try to act like they can do somethin'. Go take him, man."

I heard Tyrod talking to Zarick, as they stood a few feet away from me during recess.

So far, I'd only been to a few karate sessions, and I

hadn't learned very much. I knew Zarick had mad skills. As much as I believed in my heart that I could defend myself, I realized sometimes winning the battle is staying out of a battle you can't win. So I got up from the swing and walked in the other direction, toward the wooded area.

When I heard footsteps behind me, I realized I probably should have walked in the direction where the rest of the class was playing. But it was too late. Trying to avoid turning around to see a fist in my face, I picked up speed and kept walking toward the forest. It's a place that all students are forbidden to ever enter.

Tyrod called out, "Wait up, Jack. Where you goin'?"

"Jack's not my name," I said, as I turned around.

I kept walking, knowing Tyrod wasn't going to leave me alone. "Come here and let me talk to you. Zarick sent me to tell you somethin'."

Just wanting him to go away, I stopped and said, "Why would I want to hear anything he wants to tell me?"

"Cuz . . ."

"Whatever, Tyrod. I heard what you were sayin' to him. You were tryin' to get him to fight me and stuff."

"Aw, I was just messin' around. I was just tryin' to see if he was for real. He said he wants to be cool with you."

Shocked, I said, "He told you that?"

"Yep, yesterday. So I was just seeing if he really means it. He didn't wanna come over here and get embarrassed. He wanted to see if you were down with squashing all the trouble and y'all being cool. So what's up?"

I looked over Tyrod's shoulder and Zarick was definitely checking out our conversation. He didn't seem angry, and I certainly wasn't up to a fight.

"Wassup? What you wanna go and tell my boy? You down with y'all workin' it out?"

I nodded. Tyrod took off and ran back to Zarick. I stood there and was actually confused when Zarick looked at me real hard, balled up his fist, and started running toward me.

"What? What's the problem? What's goin' on?" I said, just as Zarick pushed me hard.

Ready to shove me again, Zarick said, "Oh, don't even trip. Don't even act like you don't know what you just said."

Tyrod jumped in and added, "Yeah, man, I asked did you think you could beat my boy fightin'. You know you nodded your head yes and said Zarick's skills are weak."

Before I could even say that it wasn't true, and Tyrod was putting words in my mouth, Tyrod started jumping up and down. He was acting as if he was in a boxing ring, trying to pump up a fight.

"I'm tryin' to work it out and have no beef with you. You're gonna talk about me like that?" Zarick said, believing Tyrod's crazy words.

"Don't you guys see what he's doin'?" Morgan said, running up behind us. I didn't even see her coming.

"Back up! Nobody's even talkin' to you, girl!" Tyrod shouted, as he turned away from her.

"He's tellin' you guys stuff to keep up trouble," Morgan

said, making sure we knew the real deal as she saw it.

"Well, when he first came over here, Tyrod did tell me that you wanted to squash everything," I said to Zarick.

"And I do."

"I told him I was down with that," I said, looking over at Tyrod. He was still up to his tricks.

"Man, you gonna lie to me like that?" Zarick said, turning to Tyrod.

"See, you guys just need to work it out and be friends," Morgan said, as she stepped between Zarick and me.

I just looked at her, really irritated. Yeah, I was scared, thinking I might have to fight Zarick. I didn't want that to happen, but at the same time, I didn't want Morgan stepping all in the middle of it either. Who needed her always trying to make things better and work out my problems? I could handle it on my own. Having no more words at the moment, I started walking away.

Zarick tried to talk to Morgan, but she followed me. I stopped walking and shouted, "Why are you doin' this? Leave me alone."

"What's wrong with you? Why are you actin' mad?" Morgan said, frowning at me.

"Because I want to handle my own problems . . . and . . . and . . . I like you! Okay?"

Walking back to the playground in a hurry, I left her standing there with her mouth wide open. I didn't want to tell her, but it was the truth. I also didn't want her to think I was a wimp who couldn't take care of my business.

• • •

"So you've been goin' to karate class for a while. He still won't let you test for the next color belt? Mr. Black has been teachin' me how to block, kick, throw, do the side step, the front step, and the back step. What've you been learnin'?" Trey asked me.

It felt like steam was shooting out of my ears. I was too embarrassed to admit I've only been doing minor stuff. I certainly wasn't getting an opportunity to really grow like Trey.

Mr. Stone seems like he doesn't want to teach me anything. Instead, he still makes me polish his floors and do simple stuff that doesn't amount to much. As bad as I want to learn the skills, my dad won't let me change gyms and instructors. It's so frustrating that I couldn't even answer Trey.

"Well, man, if I was you . . . ," Trey started giving me advice I didn't ask for. "When I go there tonight, I would demand that he test me for the next belt. What if those dudes come at you again? Are you always gonna go the other way?"

"That was two weeks ago, Trey. Zarick says he doesn't really wanna fight me anymore."

"Yeah, that's what he said then, but what happens when he changes his mind and Morgan's not there to break it up? Huh?" Trey's question made me even angrier.

At that moment, I grabbed his shirt and held it real

tight. I didn't care what karate moves he knew. He was crossing the line with me, and I could handle mine.

"That's what I'm talkin' about. That's my boy. Ah'ight. See, you need to go to that karate instructor and act like that today. Then you'll be good."

"Did you guys finish that work I gave you?" Dr. Richardson asked the two of us.

I started to sweat because I'd been staring for the longest at the exercise sheet on context clues. When she threatened to give us a zero, I knew it was time to focus.

"See, neither one of you knows what to do because you were running your mouths when I was explaining. Guess what? I'm not going over it again!" my feisty teacher said in a firm tone.

"Do you know how to do this?" Trey leaned over and whispered to me.

When I shrugged my shoulders, Trey added, "You used to know how to do everything. Now you pick the year I sit next to you to be just as pitiful as me with grades and stuff."

Hearing us still talking, Dr. Richardson asked, "Trey and Alec, do I need to send you both to the principal's office?"

Together, we said, "No, ma'am!"

That was the last thing I needed. So I started working. I did what my dad taught me to do when I was lost, I read the directions. It said context clues found in a sentence are to be used when you don't understand the meaning of a word. That means you look at the other words in the sentence and allow them to help you figure out what the words in bold mean.

For example, the first sentence read:

1. Presidents of the United States are always very **prominent** people whom we admire.

By checking out the context clues in this sentence, I had to find out the meaning of the word "prominent." Does it mean: A) unimportant, B) important, C) carefree, or D) obtuse?

Because I know from math that the word "obtuse" is an angle, I cancelled that one out right away. Reading the sentence again, I looked at the words around the bold word and noticed a clue. It said that presidents are *people whom we admire.* I didn't think those people were "unimportant" or "carefree," so I cancelled out those two choices. That left me with the right answer: B) important.

The next sentence was:

2. It was hard to understand the student's answer because she **droned** on and on just like an alarm clock that would not quit buzzing. Does the word "droned" mean: A) hummed, B) barked, C) chirped, or D) whistled?

The context clue I found for the word "droned" was: *an alarm clock that would not stop buzzing.* My clock radio has a buzzing tone when it wakes me up in the mornings, so I chose the word closest to that sound: A) hummed.

The next sentence read:

3. The **scrawny** boy was just right for the basketball team; though he wasn't big, he was all muscle. Does the word "scrawny" mean: A) large, B) thick, C) cubed, or D) lean. The clue, *"though he wasn't big,"* didn't match "large," "thick," or "cubed," so I chose the answer: D) lean.

Time was running out, and I had to turn in my paper. I had only answered three of the seven questions because I wasted so much time talking to Trey. Now I wasn't going to get a good grade, and that didn't feel good at all.

Later on that day, I was on my way to karate practice. Dad got on my case pretty bad about my academics again. "Alec, I've been giving you a chance, wanting you to pick up the pace when it comes to studying and improving your grades. So far, I haven't heard good news about this. Every time I turn around, I'm getting an e-mail from Dr. Richardson telling me you're not giving her your best effort."

Then, he gave me the worse news of all when he told me, "I'm thinking about taking you out of karate. You've been complaining about Mr. Stone and saying you don't want to be in his class anyway. But know that I'm not taking you out because that's what you want. I really don't think you deserve to be in it."

The more he talked, the more Dad was getting upset. "Ugh, boy, I'm so frustrated with you! In spite of my warnings, you're not keeping up with your chores. You know I'm dealing with all this stuff with your grandmother. Since your mom is away, I would think you'd want to help me hold things together a little bit more. For some reason, you don't want to do your part."

I wanted to say, *Dad, what else is going on with you? I haven't been all that bad.* Then again, I guess I haven't been all that good either. So I said nothing.

"Alec, I need you to straighten up right now. Please, do it for me. Just go in there and do what the man says and be a good student. Otherwise, this is it."

"You're not gonna stay?" I wanted Dad to see for himself how Mr. Stone treated me. Maybe then he'd have a better idea about the way things really are.

"No, I've got to go and pick up Grandma from the doctor's office. You'll be all right. You know how to act."

When I went inside, Mr. Stone made me run laps around the gym because I was late. It wasn't like I was driving the car. He didn't even ask me if there was something wrong that kept me from getting here on time. Last week, a guy was late, and Mr. Stone didn't make him do anything extra.

Running around the gym, I thought about all Trey said he was learning from his instructor. It was making me feel sick and tired of putting up with all this stuff.

I couldn't take it anymore, so I ran up to Mr. Stone and said, "Why won't you really teach me how to do this? Why is there all this extra stuff that makes no sense? I got a lot going on in my life, and I need to learn karate for real. I'm ready to test for the next belt, and you won't even give me a try."

Mr. Stone just looked at me real hard and said, "Oh, so

you think you're ready, huh? You think you can handle it, huh? Okay, show me what you got!" Then he took a stand like he was going to be my sparring partner.

Other kids stopped to pay attention. They started laughing as I sized up my teacher. "You're a black belt. Of course, I'm not ready to go up against you."

"You're running your mouth . . . acting like you're the instructor and know what's best," Mr. Stone said, as he grabbed me by my uniform shirt and pulled me out to the middle of the floor. He kept demanding me to show him what I had. That's when I threw a couple of punches; which, of course, went absolutely nowhere.

Thoughts were going through my mind about how messed up I felt my life was. I wasn't doing my best in school. I still really missed my mom. I was upset that my grandmother was sick. It really seemed like I was losing in every way. A yucky feeling came over me because I want to be a winner. I want things to be good. I want things to be right—and everything felt so wrong.

I was so angry that I didn't realize what I was doing anymore. So much so that I was punching and kicking at the air, until the instructor grabbed me and said, "That's right. Let it out, Alec. That's what karate really is, a sport to help you cleanse your mind. You're going to be all right."

Suddenly, a feeling of peace washed over me like I was taking a cool shower. I heard the tough guy who I thought didn't like me at all say, "Alec, quit fighting. Let it all out so you can feel better."

Letter to Mom

Dear Mom,

This is really a hard time for me. Confused by everything going on, I just have to get a handle on things. Honestly, I've been anxious to learn karate so I can be a good fighter. Dad has a lot of confidence in my karate teacher, but Mr. Stone still won't teach me.

I haven't been able to stop thinking about this situation because it's so important to me. I feel like I'm ready to try out for the next belt, but I don't know how long Mr. Stone is going to make me wait. I'm worried he won't let me.

Mom, I know I can do it. Mr. Stone doesn't seem to agree. But I have to be ready if someone at school challenges me.

Your son,
Dreaming of learning karate, Alec

Word Search:

UKE (oo-key) – BLOCKS

```
E  K  O  G  H  Y  Z  E  I  E  U  W
P  K  A  T  S  W  D  D  K  K  X  Q
S  A  U  X  M  P  J  U  M  U  G  L
R  H  O  N  E  D  E  J  H  I  K  V
U  W  U  S  A  G  H  P  C  M  O  K
F  J  F  T  A  D  S  G  E  A  S  P
M  J  Q  E  O  Y  U  U  A  S  A  H
S  J  K  Y  A  U  Y  H  K  A  U  A
J  O  D  A  N  U  K  E  C  H  K  W
F  R  V  I  S  X  M  E  N  S  E  J
T  X  L  Y  F  I  V  Z  R  I  V  Z
I  A  R  A  B  N  A  D  E  G  V  R
```

Age Uke (Ah-geh oo-key): upward block
Chudan Uke (chew-dahn oo-key): outward middle forearm block
Gedan Barai (geh-dahn bah-rye): downward block
Hasami Uke (ha-sah-may oo-key): scissor block
Jodan Uke (jo-dahn oo-key): upward block
Kosa Uke (co-sah oo-key): cross block
Shuto Uke (shoo-toh oo-key: knife hand block

Pleasant Surprise

6

"**Alec, honey, don't** cry," a sweet voice said to me. Could I be dreaming? The voice sounded so real.

I buried my head even further in the karate instructor's chest. I guess I'd been crying so long and so hard that I thought I heard my mother calling out to me. At least, I wished it were her.

Inwardly, I prayed, *"Lord, this is embarrassing. All these people are looking at me. I miss my mom so much, and I need her in my life. Wishing so bad that she was here, now I'm hearing her voice. Lately, I feel like I'm losing at every-thing, and now it seems like I'm losing my mind. Hearing my mom's voice? What's wrong with me? Help me, please."*

The instructor gently separated the two of us, placed his hands on my shoulders, and turned me around. "Son," he said, "I think someone is here that you want to see."

When I lifted my head and opened my eyes it wasn't a

dream after all. It was my beautiful mother standing in front of me with her arms open wide! Just like that, my prayer was answered, and God took away my pain! I leaped into her arms and hugged her so tight!

As excited as if I'd scored a touchdown, I shouted, "Mom! I can't believe you're here! Oh, my goodness! When did you get here? This can't be true, but you're standing right here. I'm hugging you, I'm touching you! Mom! . . . "

"Calm down, son," she said with a huge smile. "Yes, it's me."

I stepped away from her and asked in a voice that was sad again, "When are you going back?"

"No worries, Alec, honey. I'm here for a couple of months. The show is on hiatus. We're taking a nice long break."

While Mom said a few words to the karate instructor, I went to the dressing room to change out of my uniform. Still hoping this wasn't a dream, I changed in record time.

As we were driving along, Mom started buttering me up real good, telling me how much she missed me. She was letting me know how much fun we were going to have while she was home. Then she asked me if I was hungry. As we sat eating our burgers, fries, and shakes, she just kept looking at me. I know I'm not a detective, but that made me suspicious.

So I took another sip of my shake and asked, "What's goin' on, Mom?"

"I want you to talk to me, Alec. But, I don't want to push you. You'll open up when you're ready, but it's been an hour, and you haven't said a word about why you were in tears at the karate school."

"You mean, Dad didn't tell you what's been goin' on?"

"I need you to tell me in your own words, honey."

All of a sudden, my appetite was gone. I'd been writing my mom letters, but hadn't sent some of them because I didn't want her to worry. Besides that, it was hard to explain how much pressure there's been on me. I wasn't sure how to say it. But I could see from her teary eyes that she didn't want me hurting, and she was here to help me get better.

So I said, "I don't know, Mom. It's this guy at school . . . Zarick, one of the boys I've written to you about . . . " Then my voice trailed off. I looked away because I couldn't finish.

She touched my hand and said, "He's been giving you trouble? Has he been bullying you? Does he want to fight?"

"I actually don't think he wants to fight anymore. At least, that's what he told me. But he likes Morgan," I said in a pitiful voice.

Mom asked, "Morgan? The young lady from our neighborhood?"

"Yes, ma'am."

She didn't say anything and neither did I. I just hung my head low and stared at the fries on my plate that were getting cold.

"It bothers you that he likes Morgan, huh?"

"Yeah, and I don't understand why. I mean, I don't like girls. Morgan's my buddy, but I can't explain it."

She giggled a little bit at that.

"Mom, it's not funny!"

She replied, "No, you're just growing up and things are happening to you that you can't explain. Well, it's not a bad thing that you really care about her. But you do have to understand something, Alec. You're young now, but don't ever be the type of guy who doesn't like somebody because you think they're standing in your way. Do you understand what I'm saying, son? Maybe this Zarick guy and you could be friends. Forget how he feels about Morgan. She's your buddy. You're right about that. However, you can't control who she hangs out with and you certainly can't be upset when other people think she's just as cool as you do. So are you going to try it?"

"Try what?" I asked in a shocked tone, knowing that she couldn't mean what I thought she meant. "You mean, be Zarick's friend? No way!"

"Just be open-minded about it. Okay, son? In order to be successful in life and solve problems, you have to see things a different way. In other words, if you want to get different results, you must do something different. Thinking this young man is your enemy hasn't been working. It's driving you crazy! So release all of that. You never know what could happen between the two of you. It could be a positive thing," she said, as I frowned. "What else is up?"

"Well, you know I've missed you."

"I've missed you too, Alec, and that's why I'm here. I love you. You know that. So we'll work on us. I'm going to be spending a lot of 'Mommy and Alec' time, along with spending a lot of 'Mommy and Antoine' time. Is that cool? I still want to cuddle you because you're still my baby."

Letting her know I was tough, I said, "I'm growin' up, Mom."

"You're still my baby," she repeated in a soft tone, as she pinched both my cheeks.

"Ouch!" I protested.

"And Grandma . . . how's Grandma?" asked Mom.

I shrugged my shoulders and said, "Oh, yeah. I'm really glad you're here, Mom. Dad needs you. We need you. Grandma needs you."

"She's a strong woman. I don't know why some things happen in life, but I do know that God is good. He helps us through our hard times."

I'd never heard that before, but Mom told me that it was in the Bible. It was a comforting thought and a real treat. Sort of like the hot fudge sundae she bought me later that day.

Spending time with my mom was something I desperately needed to do. While enjoying that yummy treat, we had another opportunity to talk about my problems. Life was looking up after all.

● ● ●

"Now, Alec, you know I only let one of my students take a washroom break at a time. Why are you standing at my desk, asking to go like you're a kindergartener?" Dr. Richardson said to me, as I stood in front of her, shaking like a leaf in the wind.

I was so focused on my work that I hadn't even paid attention when another classmate asked to go. Standing in the front of the class, I scanned the room and noticed Zarick's desk was empty. The last person in the world I wanted be alone with in the washroom was Zarick. I still didn't know where he was coming from, and I certainly didn't want any fights to start. But I had to go and couldn't hold it any longer.

"Please, Dr. Richardson."

"Hurry up!" She said in one of those tones like, *you're getting on my nerves, but I'll let you go anyway* voice.

I couldn't take my time if I wanted to. Although I really wanted Zarick out of the washroom, he wasn't coming out soon enough. As I tiptoed in, I was really surprised by what I heard. Someone was moaning and it sounded like Zarick's voice. As quietly as I could, I peered around the corner. Right away, I saw a shocking sight that actually scared me.

Zarick was standing in the mirror, holding his shirt up on the right side. He was looking at the deepest, red bruise I had ever seen. Part of me wanted to ask him, *Are you okay? What happened? Do you need some help?* But before I could say anything, he took his left fist and hit the wall so hard that he slid down to the floor. That was even more shocking.

Not only did I think Zarick would be the one to give somebody a bruise and not get one, but I never thought I'd see him cry. The guy started wailing pretty loud. Since he wasn't in the nurse's clinic, in my dad's office, or talking to Dr. Richardson outside of her classroom door, it was clear that he wanted to keep whatever was going on a secret.

As he got up and splashed water on his face, I jetted out the door so that when he exited he wouldn't even know I was there.

Hurrying back to the classroom before Dr. Richardson came looking for me, I prayed, *"Lord, maybe this is what Mom was talkin' about. She told me to be more open to people. We shouldn't really judge others because we don't know what folks have going on in their lives. Honestly, I'm not sayin' that I want to be Zarick's friend, but I will ask You to help him. And if I'm supposed to do more, please show me how. From what I just saw, he doesn't want anybody in his business. One thing is for sure, he needs You. Amen."*

About twenty minutes later, Dr. Richardson gave us an assignment. We were going to have to do a paper, and we needed partners. When she called out the pairs, she teamed me up with Zarick! Maybe I did have a good connection with the Lord and He was about to answer my prayer. If I was going to be working with Zarick, surely we would get to know each other better.

I didn't mean to set out to be his partner. There was no way for me to know this was about to happen. God worked that out. Could it be that God was telling me that He needed me to step up and help? However, I admit I was bit resistant when Zarick looked over at me and frowned. I sighed.

Tyrod quickly raised his hand and said, "Dr. Richardson, why can't I be partners with Zarick?"

"Watch your tone, young man, or you're going to be partners with Dr. London in his office. How about that?" replied Dr. Richardson.

The class burst out laughing.

Tyrod wouldn't let up. "I don't wanna be partners with Trey."

Trey spoke up and said, "I don't wanna be partners with him either."

"Well, the list is done and unless you both want to get Fs, you'll figure it out. I'll give the class a few minutes to get into your groups and come up with a topic, which I need to approve. The paper needs to be about 'contrast and comparison.' Can anyone describe what I'm talking about?" Dr. Richardson asked, as Morgan raised her hand. "Yes, Morgan?"

"When you talk about contrast, that's when two subjects are different. But also in the paper you want us to do a comparison. That would show how the two subjects are alike."

"That's exactly right," Dr. Richardson said, "I want this

to be a four paragraph paper. You need to write an opening paragraph, a paragraph on how the topics are alike, a paragraph on how they are different, and the closing paragraph."

When Zarick and I got together, he looked at me, and I looked at him. Neither of us wanted to talk. He didn't know what I was thinking and probably assumed I didn't want to work with him. Even though I had my doubts, I would take my mom's advice and try to be open.

"Well, we've got to come up with a topic," he said.

"What about bumps and bruises? We can write about them," I said, thinking back to when I saw him in the washroom.

"Why would you wanna write about that?" Zarick asked in a defensive tone, as his eyes widened.

Looking away so he wouldn't know there was more to it, I responded, "Hmmm, I don't know. In football, we get bumps and bruises all the time."

"Well, I don't like football, basketball, or baseball."

"I don't like baseball either," I said to him. "But actually, I played during the summer, and it wasn't that bad." Next, I suggested, "We can write about a family, I guess."

"I don't wanna write about no family," Zarick quickly said.

"Well, I've been takin' karate lessons," I uttered, knowing that was a sport we had in common.

"You know I love karate. Even though I'm trained not to use what I know, sometimes I really want to," Zarick said. Then I kind of thought maybe he would open up and tell me what was going on, but he didn't.

"Yeah. So what can we compare and contrast to karate?"

"Somethin' similar, but not the same," said Zarick.

"I got it! What about boxing? Do you like that? There's a big match comin' up, and my dad's excited about it. Maybe you can come over and watch it with us."

Zarick's eyebrows raised high. "You'd let me come over to your house?"

"Why not? We have to work on this paper. I don't know much about boxing. It's sort of like karate, but definitely different. For instance, you have to use gloves in boxing, but not in karate."

Zarick didn't respond to that and seemed focused on something entirely different. "I'm just surprised you want me to come over. That's really cool, man, after all we've been through. I think I'm gonna like bein' your partner."

When I saw him smile, I smiled too. Even better, Dr. Richardson approved our topic on karate and boxing.

● ● ●

"Man, this boxing match is great!" Zarick said to me. We were watching the big fight on TV and munching on some snacks my mom prepared for us.

"I'm glad you could come over."

"Yeah, it's been cool. I know I've been mean to you. Since it was a new class, I just wanted to try and act cool.

Whatever Tyrod said to do, I would do it, just like I was his puppet. I shouldn't have done that. I'm real sorry."

"I owe you an apology too."

"For what? I was the one being mean to you," Zarick said.

"Yeah, but I could have talked to you instead of letting Tyrod get in the middle of the two of us."

My mother popped into the family room and said, "Alec, son, may I see you for a second?"

"Yes, ma'am," I called out to her. Looking at Zarick's empty cup, I asked him, "You want me to get you some more soda?"

"Yeah, that's cool."

I went into the kitchen, and Mom had this huge smile on her face. "You made a new friend! This is so cool. We had a conversation about you being open. Now he's over here, and you guys are having a good time! Great! I'm so happy it's working out," she said, as she pinched my cheeks. Again.

"Mom!"

"Okay. I just wanted to tell you how proud I am of you. When we talked last week about making friends with Zarick, it was the last thing on your mind. Now look at you two."

"He's not my best friend or anything. But . . . something's changed," I replied, thinking back to seeing Zarick in the school washroom.

The thought of him hurting badly and crying wasn't

cool. I still hadn't brought up the subject with Zarick. At the same time, I felt I couldn't tell Mom about it either.

"You guys go and work on your paper. I know you're doing the right thing. When you can make your enemies your friends, Alec, you'll go far in this life."

"Yes, Mom."

Zarick and I worked for almost two hours. I wanted him to open up to me about what was going on. I noticed him grabbing his side and wincing from time to time. But when I looked at him with a question on my face, he just said that he was tired and brushed it off. Sometimes he pretended like he didn't see me looking.

Then, out of nowhere, our conversation went deeper when we started talking about Morgan.

"I know you care a lot about Morgan Love," he said to me.

"I mean, I've known her for a few years. She lives right down the street. She's my girl. You know, like my buddy," I tried to explain.

"Naw, you like her. You didn't like it when I thought she was really cool. Then I backed away because I didn't really understand what I was feeling."

I said, "Yeah, I really think I do like her. I mean . . . I don't know how to describe it."

"You don't have to. I'm stayin' away because she made it plain to me that she thinks you're cooler than I am."

"Really?" I said, smiling wider than a big screen TV.

"Yep, hopefully she and I can be friends, though. I

want you and me to be friends too. I've learned a lot from my mom and her relationships since my dad left. People shouldn't try and force something, if it's not right."

I didn't know what he was talking about, but it sounded deep. We gave each other a fist bump and just left it at that.

Zarick and I weren't real tight, but we'd been spending time together when we had breaks to work on our paper. There was a lot to do. First, we went to the library to check out a couple of books for research on our subject. Next, we had to write the first and second draft. Then we used the computer in the technology lab to type it up and get it ready.

One day, at lunchtime, we were going over our paper. While sitting together and talking about our work, Tyrod came up from behind us and said, "Wassup, Zarick! I can't believe you're sittin' here with this loser. Man, you were just talkin' about him when we were in the lunch line."

I gave Tyrod a look like *go and sit down somewhere, nobody's tryin' to hear what you've gotta say.* He wasn't going to get me to fall for his tricks anymore. Zarick looked like he wanted Tyrod to be quiet and go away too. For Tyrod, that was impossible.

He looked straight at Zarick. "Didn't you just say that hangin' out with this dude wasn't all you thought it was cracked up to be?"

Zarick replied, "First off, you're takin' it . . . "

I did a double take and said, "Wait, did you say bein'

with me wasn't all it was cracked up to be?"

"Yeah, I said that. But I didn't mean . . . "

Zarick was starting to trip over his words. It made me wonder if maybe he was talking about me behind my back.

"Mmm hmm. You got doubts now. Right, Alec? This little partnership you thought you had with my boy. Please! It ain't real. We talk about you every time you ain't around," added Tyrod.

"That's not true. I don't even hang out with you anymore, and you know it."

"Whatever. You came over to my house after you watched boxing at his house, didn't you?"

Of course, it was okay for Zarick to go wherever he wanted to go. I wasn't his mom or his babysitter. But I didn't want anybody to play me by making me think we're cool when that wasn't the case.

Tyrod teased, "You know you just wanted to be his partner so you could get an A on the assignment and not do any of the work."

Me and Zarick looked at each other. I didn't know what he was thinking, but I was really hoping I wasn't being used.

Tyrod kept it up. "Okay. Who's typin' the paper?"

I didn't answer, but it was me.

"Who read the book that you checked out from the library and then wrote up the information about it?"

Again, I didn't answer. But the answer was me.

"Who wrote the two drafts? It wasn't Zarick. So somebody's gettin' played!" Then he laughed right in my face.

That's when Zarick let him have it. "You know what? I'm sick and tired of you tellin' me what you think you know—when you don't know nothin'! I said bein' at his house wasn't all it was cracked up to be because it was way more than I thought it would be. I came over to your house after I left his house to get my jacket that you kept forgettin' to bring to school. I'd been askin' for it about a month.

Oh, this is great, I thought to myself. Tyrod was at it again, but this time Zarick stood up to him and said, "You just can't deal with the fact that I've got somebody else I'm hangin' out with. Yeah, I might not be as smart as Alec, but every step of the way I've been with him learnin', workin', and givin' my two-cents to what we're doin'. So step on off, Tyrod! Get on out of the way and quit tryin' to mess up our chance to be real friends. You're just sayin' all this stuff because you're jealous that nobody even wants to be your friend."

Tyrod was speechless. He just dropped his head and walked away. Zarick didn't have to say anything more. He wasn't trying to boast about putting Tyrod in his place. But I'm sure he felt good that he wasn't letting Tyrod walk all over him. I was happy he stood up to Tyrod and set the record straight. We both just smiled. Wow! Zarick didn't let Tyrod win. What a pleasant surprise!

Letter to Mom

Dear Mom,

I thought I was hallucinating when I saw you. You are really here, and I'm so happy! I'm glad your show is taking a break. The time we're spending together is so great. You probably already know that I won't like it when you go back.

Mom, your advice was right on time! Thanks for helping out with things between Zarick and me. We're getting along just fine now. I can't help but boast because you've got it going on! Taking your advice really worked.

Your son,
Smiling 'cuz you're home, Alec

Word Search:

GERI WAZA (geh-rhee wah-zah)
KICKING TECHNIQUES

```
G U W A M K G K V P G I
N P J X E S O E U O R R
T J B A P Q F G D E K E
U N G E Y Y S Z G N E G
M E F U M A K O M I K U
F A I R E G R X Q E O S
S K E M W I E L E T M T
E C U G H O C L G O I E
Z F Z S E R B E T P V S
J U U Q J R F I H U W N
A P A B A E I W Z Z A A
D O Q Z O V E C W P I K
```

Geri (geh-rhee): kick
Fumakomi (foo-mah-ko-mee): side stomp kick
Kansetsu Geri (can-set-sue geh-rhee): kicks aimed at joints
Keage (key-ah-gay): snap
Kekomi (key-ko-mee): thrust
Mae Geri (mah-eh geh-rhee): front kick
Ushiro Geri (oo-she-row geh-rhee): back kick

Life's Battle

7

"**Oh, Alec! You** got these flowers for me?" Morgan asked, as I handed her a couple of pink roses. Mom let me take them from an arrangement she bought for our kitchen table.

"It's just somethin' I got from the house."

"Still . . . this is so special," Morgan said, as she took them with a big smile. "Why are you giving me these?"

I didn't know what to say. I looked everywhere but at her. My hands started sweating. I was so nervous.

Finally, our eyes met, and I managed to say, "Because I think you're awesome, and I just wanted you to know it."

"But you don't like me or anything. You said so," she said, remembering what I told her at the beginning of the school year.

"Well, I don't give flowers to people I don't like."

Before she could say anything else, I quickly turned around and took off. I guess I was either walking too fast or my timing wasn't right. Just then, Dad stepped out of his office. He didn't look too happy with me.

In a stern voice, he said, "Okay, you're safety patrol. You're supposed to be setting an example, son. What's your hurry?"

As soon as Dad looked over my shoulder, he smiled and turned me around. We both saw Morgan standing there with the sweetest smile on her face, clutching the flowers.

I was worried what Dad would say when he found out, but I was prepared to tell him that Mom said it was okay. Then Dad surprised me when all he said was, "My boy! Go on to your post. And slow down in the hallway." I couldn't help but notice the silly grin he was wearing.

Heading to take up my post near the boys' washroom in the fifth grade hall, I heard Tyrod's loud laugh. When I saw him standing with Zarick, he wasn't acting friendly.

"You look so silly," Tyrod teased. "What? You mean, you can't protect yourself anymore, karate boy? Martial arts not workin' out for you? Look at you. You got a busted lip."

"Just leave me alone, man. Okay?" Zarick said to him.

Looking at it, I had to admit, Zarick's lip was torn up. It was all red and puffy and swollen.

"Boy, you look so bad. Maybe you should've stayed home," Tyrod joked.

Zarick said, "Well, it wasn't that bad when I left the house."

As I stood there listening, I thought to myself, *I don't know how bad it was when you left the house, but your lip is pretty messed up now.* I had a feeling as soon as Dr. Richardson took a look at it, she'd be sending him straight to the office.

Tyrod just kept picking at him and making jokes until I could tell it was getting on Zarick's nerves. All of a sudden, he stood right in front of Tyrod with his fist in Tyrod's face.

Zarick raised his voice and said, "I don't have no problem makin' your lip look worse than mine. You wanna try me?"

"Naw, naw, my bad, my bad," Tyrod responded. He threw his hands up in the air and stepped away.

When Tyrod was gone, Zarick turned and put his face against the wall. I was hoping he wasn't going to cry. It was plain to see that my new buddy was having a hard time.

Walking up behind him, I put my hand on his back and said, "Talk to me, man. What's goin' on?" When Zarick gave me no answer, I patted his back as gently as I could. "It's gonna be okay. It's gonna be okay."

I guess I must have pressed too hard or something because Zarick pulled away. "Ouch! Man, that hurt!" he cried out.

"I'm sorry, man. How can I help?"

But Zarick just walked off, not wanting to deal with answering my question. By then, it was pretty late. But, I took my post by the door. Soon, the bell rang, and I headed to class.

Moments later, Zarick walked into the classroom.

Dr. Richardson took one look at him and walked him back out into the hallway so they could talk in private. I don't know what he told her, but a few minutes later, he came back in with a paper towel in his hand and sat down.

She must not have thought it was serious enough to make him go the office and get help. Help that I knew he needed. In less than two weeks time, Zarick had a deep bruise on his stomach and now a busted lip. It was pretty plain to me that something was wrong.

One thing's for sure, Zarick wasn't doing this to himself. Somebody's been hurting him. It wasn't right for him to keep it all in just to protect the person who was causing him so much pain. I was happy when we got to break up into groups and do some final work on our papers. They were due today, and I needed to talk to Zarick.

It wasn't as easy as I thought to bring all this up, so I just stared at him. "What? What do you wanna ask me? What do you wanna know?"

Finally, here was my opening, so I went for it. "What's goin' on with you, man? I saw you in the washroom one day, and you had the worst bruise on your stomach that I'd ever seen. Now, it's your lip. And you felt pain in your back when I touched it. What's goin' on? Who hurt you?"

"My mom . . . "

"Your mom did this to you?"

"No, she's dating this man. When she goes to work at night she leaves us with him. For no reason at all, he starts swinging at me. He was gonna hit my little sister yesterday, and I stepped in. That's when he punched me in the mouth. The other day, he hit me in the back and it's still sore."

"You've gotta talk to somebody about this!"

"No, no, no. I can't. He's helpin' my mom pay bills. She really cares about him. She told me that she didn't wanna mess this up. So I'm just thinkin' if he hits me one more time, I'm gonna use all the karate stuff I know. And it's not gonna be pretty."

Scratching my head in disbelief, I said, "But I gotta say somethin'."

Quickly his eyes narrowed, and he replied, "If you do, we'll never be friends again. I trusted you with this. Okay? Now let's just practice the speech that we're gonna give when we talk about our paper." Zarick then pointed to his lip and added, "Forget about this. This is my problem."

Feeling the weight of it all, I said, "If you need me . . . "

"I know you're there." Zarick finished my sentence, reached over and put his hand on my shoulder, and nodded.

After lunch, Dr. Richardson called Zarick and me up to the front of the room. It was time for us to read our paper to the class.

KARATE VS. BOXING

Karate and boxing are two types of fighting sports. There are some similarities in the way that both sports are carried out. Both sports are meant to punish whoever steps up to fight. The difference in the two sports is in the way the participants fight. Boxers use special gloves and have to follow certain rules in order to win a belt and prizes. Those who know Karate get to show off their skills by following some important rules as well. We think both sports are cool.

Boxing and Karate are similar in a few ways, but not many. Karate is a group of primarily striking-based martial arts styles that come from Japan. On the other hand, Boxing is a man-to-man combat. The two types of fighting both inflict pain on their opponent. Both sports are combat sports and are for tough people.

However, Karate and boxing are different as well. Karate is mainly used for self-defense, and it is a great stress reliever. Two boxers fight to see who is the strongest and can win. Karate is a fighting art too, and it also has some sport aspects. Karate uses both hands and feet, as opposed to boxing, which only uses hands while fighting. Boxing is fought with boxing gloves that cover the entire fist to protect the hands. Other than hands and feet, Karate doesn't use any other equipment while fighting. Boxing is held in a ring with four sides, while on the other hand, karate is done on a special floor mat.

In the sport of fighting, boxing and karate are two of the top ones. They might not have much in common, but the one thing they do have in common is that they both can cause pain. There are several ways that these sports are different such as the way they are fought, where the two fights happen, what they fight on, and the fighting styles. Boxing and Karate are tough sports that are exciting.

By Alec and Zarick

Dr. Richardson was very impressed. She gave both Zarick and me an A. That pumped me up, and Zarick felt good too. We both smiled and gave each a high five. Wow, what a relief!

● ● ●

Things were finally looking up! I went to practice feeling really good. Dad wasn't threatening to take me out of karate anymore. Mom talked him into giving me another chance.

It was a relief to become friends with someone who was once my enemy. Besides that, some other good things were happening. I finally let Morgan know that I really do care about her. And my grades were improving! Not too shabby, huh?

One thing is best of all, I'm sure my life is better because Mom's been home. Seeing her every day makes me feel like I'm on top of the world.

When I arrived at the gym, Mr. Stone was standing outside by the front door. It seemed like he was waiting for me. He had a smile on his face, which was very unusual for a man who is always so tough.

"Good to see you, Alec. I have some good news for you today."

Good news? I thought to myself. *Wow, cool.*

"You've been asking and asking when you are going to test for your next belt. Well, today's the day."

At that moment, I froze. My eyes got real big, and my mouth dropped open. He hadn't told me that I was going to test today. I wasn't prepared. I wasn't ready. I was nervous. I turned around and tried to catch Mom before she pulled off so that I could go back home.

Mr. Stone grabbed my arm and said, "Oh, no you don't. You've been wanting this. You can do it, Alec. Of all the students I've ever had, you're the one who reminds me of David from the Bible . . . little David, that is."

"I don't know what you're talkin' about, sir."

"You've never heard the story of David and Goliath?" He said to me, as we walked inside the martial arts center.

I shook my head. I wasn't thinking about a Bible story. I was thinking about the fact that I had asked for an opportunity to get the next color belt. And now that it was time, I just knew I was going to fail. Half of winning any battle is having the belief that you can. Not really wanting to admit I was afraid, fear was staring me in the face.

Mr. Stone kept talking. "Let me tell you a quick story of David and Goliath. You ready?" I didn't think I had any choice, so I nodded yes. He continued, "There was this young boy named David. His father sent him to take meals to his brothers who were fighting against the Philistine army. One day, David overheard a big guy shouting and making fun of the soldiers so he asked his brothers who the man was. That's when he learned about the mighty warrior named, Goliath. No one could defeat him, but David wasn't frightened. Then King Saul heard that there was a young man who wasn't afraid. So David had to go and see the king."

"Oh, no! He was going to fight a giant?" I asked

"Exactly. David went to the king and told him not to worry, that he would fight the giant. Even though King Saul could tell David wasn't scared, he said, 'But, you're only a boy.' David told him that he'd already killed a lion and a bear to protect his father's sheep. Deep down inside, he believed that God would help him kill the giant too.

"So the king gave David some armor to wear and weapons to use. There was only one problem—it was all too big for David. He still wasn't afraid. He was going to fight the giant without any armor. On the way, he stopped by a stream and picked up some stones and put them in his bag.

"When Goliath saw the little boy with the stones, he laughed and said, 'How are you going to come to me like this?' And David told him, 'I come to you with the Lord Almighty in this battle.' David put a stone in his slingshot, swung it around and it smacked Goliath right in the forehead. The giant fell to the ground. David won because he believed in God. And God showed up to help him."

Hearing that story, I was amazed.

"Where is this found in the Bible?" I asked, wanting to read the whole thing when I got home.

"It's from First Samuel, chapter seventeen."

"Thanks for telling me that story."

"Did you get anything out of it?" Mr. Stone asked me.

"It's kinda funny that your name is Mr. Stone and David killed Goliath with a slingshot and a stone."

Mr. Stone smiled. "That's probably one of the reasons why I really like it too."

"What else did you get from what I just told you?"

"That the Lord is always on our side, and He can help us fight any battle. If you believe that, then you can do it."

"Exactly! So sometimes I see you in church smiling like you know that the Lord is real. Is that what you think, Alec?"

"Yes, sir. I do. And I've been meanin' to tell you something. It's about the guy at school who really knows a lot about karate. At first, I wanted to learn it so I could beat him up. But you told me that wasn't the real reason I needed karate. Well, he and I are cool now."

"See there, you are so much like David. A young man who isn't afraid to step out because you believe you're never alone. You step out there with God on your side. Now, it's time for you to test for this next belt. You can do it. Are you ready?"

I smiled and said a quick prayer for strength. Then I

was ready, so I took my stance. As soon as Mr. Stone asked me to do a certain movement, I hit it exactly. Also, he gave me a certain number of push-ups, sit-ups, squat kicks from the sitting position, and squat kicks from the standing position.

Looking at Mr. Stone, I was pleased that he was smiling. I felt confident all the while I was testing and doing what he asked. I just kept thinking about David fighting Goliath.

I thought about every time I called on God to help me, and He was there. When I needed to have strength because Mom wasn't with me, God gave it to me. Thinking about that, I did a high kick.

When I didn't need to lose my temper and get into a fight at school, He helped me. I did my sit-ups, thinking about all that and how Zarick and I even became friends with God's help.

When I didn't think I could focus on my grades anymore, God helped me to know that all I needed to do was study, focus on Him, and try my best. My grades improved. Being reminded of that, I was able to do a low kick in a spin.

Before I knew it, I was done. "How'd I do?" I asked.

Mr. Stone didn't say a word. He just walked away from me and went into his office. When he returned again, he pulled a yellow belt from behind his back.

"You did great!"

All the training that he took me through, all that hard

work of rubbing polish off and on Mr. Stone's floors, really did have a purpose. I could hit the punching bag. I could do the fundamentals. I still had a long way to go, but once I realized that I had to get out of my own way, things got much better. This was a lesson I knew I could never forget.

"Thank you, sir," I said to him, as I bowed with a big smile.

"Thank you! You are one of my prize pupils," Mr. Stone said, as he proudly handed me the prized yellow belt.

● ● ●

"Oh, man, Alec! You've gotta help me. He's gone crazy. He's losin' it. I'm scared!" Zarick said in a high-pitched voice. I almost didn't recognize it was him on the phone.

"Okay, I'm gonna go and tell my dad—"

He cut me off. "No, no, no, no, no! Just pray for me! Just . . . just . . . you can't tell anybody! No one can—"

Before Zarick could finish what he was saying, I heard a ton of background noise. It sounded like chairs flying and glass breaking. Before I knew it, Zarick slammed down the phone. I was so worried. It almost felt like my heart stopped.

Quickly, I prayed, *"Lord, You've gotta help me. I don't know what to do. This is too serious, and I know I'm supposed to tell somebody. I should have told somebody everything I knew a long time ago. Now Zarick's in danger, and he still doesn't want me to tell. I asked You to make a way if*

I was supposed to hang out with him, and You did. Lord, I need You to show me what to do now. Zarick is in trouble. Show me how to help my friend and still keep his trust. Please help, Lord."

When I was getting up off my knees, my father stopped by my door and said, "Prayer time is good, but I couldn't help but overhear you say 'please help.' What's going on, son? Are you all right?"

Not sure of what to say, I didn't answer him right away. Watching me pace the floor, Dad could sense something was wrong. "All right, Alec, talk to me," he said, as his tone turned serious.

"Dad, it's one of my classmates, the guy who used to hang out with Tyrod."

"The tall, athletic looking boy who came over to watch the boxing match with you?"

"Yes, sir. That's him, Zarick."

"What's going on? What about him?"

"Dad, I should have come to you before . . . "

"Tell me what's going on, son. It's okay. Just talk to me."

"But . . . but . . . he told me not to tell you about this. That's why I didn't."

"It's okay, son. Now, tell me what's happening," Dad said, as he clearly wanted to help and not be upset with me. I wanted to make sure he understood why I didn't tell what I knew in the first place.

"Son, I'm going to say it one more time. Talk to me."

Like a balloon that suddenly burst, I let out all that was on my heart. "I was in the washroom one day at school, and I saw Zarick looking in the mirror. Dad, he had this big, red bruise on his stomach, like around his rib cage. It was bad and he was in a lot of pain. Then he hit the wall. But I didn't say anything to him right then because we weren't friends for most of the year. Right after that happened, Dr. Richardson put us together to work on this project. That's when we started to know each other. He didn't know that I knew something had happened. I mean, he takes karate. He used to threaten most of us in the class that he could beat us up. At first, I thought somebody finally gave him a piece of his own medicine. But Dad, that wasn't it."

"Okay then, what is going on?"

"Well, he came to school the other day with a busted lip and I guess some kind of other bruise or gash or something on his back. He finally told me that it's his mom's boyfriend. And Dad, he just called! He's in trouble right now!"

"What did he say, son?"

"Zarick told me that he needed my help. But, when I told him I was going to tell you, he screamed out 'no!' Then I heard all kinds of noise in the background. Scary sounds, Dad. I think he's in serious trouble. That man was yelling real loud. I've already seen some of Zarick's bruises, and that's why I'm worried."

Dad dashed out of my room. I followed him to his

home office. I watched him make a couple phone calls and then get his stuff to leave.

As he headed toward the door, I said, "Dad, I want to go. Zarick called me. He needs me. Zarick's finally reachin' out because he's in big trouble. At least, I want to explain why I didn't keep his secret. Please, Dad, please let me go!"

Dad told Mom all that was going on. She gave me a big hug and said, "I knew the Lord could help you to help others."

"I just hope I'm not too late, Mom."

Dad said, "All right, son, let's go."

We didn't say anything as we drove along, until I asked him, "Are you disappointed in me that I kept this all to myself."

"No, son, I'm disappointed in myself for not being the kind of father that you think you could come to with situations like this. I am the principal of the school, and I do recognize that somehow puts you in an uncomfortable position. We've got a whole semester to go, and I want you to know that I'm on your side. I'm not against you. I need to be the best principal that I can be. It's a good thing for me to have a son who's a student. I want you to let me know when there's something going on I need to help with."

As we got closer to Zarick's house, we heard sirens. When we pulled up, it was amazing to see a fire truck and police cars out front.

"Oh no, Dad! What's goin' on?" I yelled out, hoping

and praying that everything was okay.

Flames were coming out of one side of the house. When my dad got out of the car, I opened the passenger door and started to get out. Quickly, he told me to close it and stay inside.

I prayed, *"I know, Lord, I'm always asking for You to help me with one thing or show me how to do another. Well, right now I just need You to help my friend. Please, Lord."*

I sat there, watching the scene in front of me. In the midst of all the chaos, Zarick came running out of the house. Right behind him, his mother and little sister were escorted out by police. They all seemed okay. Finally, this man who had to be the mother's boyfriend was fighting the police as they brought him out in handcuffs.

I yelled out, "Zarick!"

When he ran over to me, Dad said it was okay for me to get out of the car.

"I'm so sorry. I'm so sorry. I had to tell," I said, thinking that my new friend was going to be mad at me.

Surprisingly, he put his hand on my shoulder and said, "I'm glad you told somebody. It was really scary. But because you cared, everything is okay."

After my dad made sure the family was fine and we were driving back home, he looked over at me and said, "Son, I'm really proud of you."

"I'm not, Dad. I should have said something a long time ago."

"Well, what matters most is that you did the right thing when you needed to."

"I don't understand how adults can be so mean sometimes."

"All adults aren't like that, son," my father explained. "But life can be tough. As long as you do the right thing and do what the Bible says, you'll make it through okay. Always remember, the rough stuff may come. But in the end, it will make you stronger. So keep doing your best and you'll see yourself winning life's battle."

Letter to Mom

Dear Mom,

I'm so glad you're home. I can share my great news with you. I'm on the right track again in school! I am studying hard and seeing good results. Dr. Richardson says she is proud of all her students. And Mom, I passed the test for my yellow belt in karate too!

Because you helped me, I am no longer afraid of Zarick. We worked everything out and are actually becoming buddies. In fact, Zarick realized he could talk to me. He told me that an adult had been abusing him physically. He didn't want me to tell anyone, but I had to break his confidence and tell Dad.

Thankfully, everything is okay with home, Zarick, and school. I know that God loves me, and I love myself enough to stay positive and do the right things.

Your son,
Winning life's battles, Alec

Word Search:
Color Belts

```
C  W  A  E  B  L  W  E  J  U  V  J
S  B  H  R  I  O  P  U  R  P  L  E
L  E  O  I  L  T  E  Z  J  A  B  T
F  W  F  L  T  M  O  S  L  D  B  C
N  Y  E  Y  B  E  G  C  O  Y  G  L
L  Y  K  C  A  L  B  J  J  Y  R  X
G  E  M  N  X  S  K  F  N  E  E  N
D  V  I  H  T  L  L  M  C  P  E  R
U  E  M  Q  F  H  A  J  F  T  N  G
V  T  R  M  K  P  U  P  E  Y  A  S
X  W  D  T  T  Q  D  E  V  Y  I  J
Y  M  W  E  R  J  M  X  S  O  B  M
```

White
Yellow
Green
Purple
Brown
Black
Red

WINNING THE BATTLE

Stephanie Perry Moore & Derrick Moore
Discussion Questions

1. Alec London is on safety patrol duty and sees tough boys doing the wrong thing. Even though Alec is a bit afraid to step in, did he do the right thing by talking to Tyrod and Zarick? How do you handle being intimidated?

2. Alec's dad asks him to open up and tell him what is on his mind. Do you think it would have helped Alec to share his feelings? Do you open up and share your feelings with your parents?

3. Alec is asked questions in class that he can't answer because he was asleep. Do you think Alec deserved to get in trouble because he wasn't paying attention? What is the best way to ensure you are always ready to give all of your attention to learning when you are in class?

4. When Grandma goes to the doctor, she learns she has cancer. Do you feel Alec should be sad? When someone you love is hurting, how can you help them deal with a painful situation?

5. When Alec is on the playground, Tyrod pits Zarick and Alec against each other. Do you think Alec should have believed what Tyrod told him about Zarick? Why is it important to go to someone directly

when you have a problem with them instead of allowing another person to speak for you?

6. When Alec went to the washroom in school, he noticed Zarick had a bruised rib. Do you think Alec should have told an adult what he saw right way? What would you do if you were concerned for your classmate?

7. Alec is afraid to compete for his next karate belt. Do you think hearing the story of David and Goliath helped him gain confidence? What did you learn from the story of David and Goliath?

Context Clues

Direction: In the sentences below, use all the words to find the meaning of the word in bold.

EXAMPLE: The spirited and active football player did fifty sit-ups. _____

A) dangerous B) energetic C) slow D) tired

ANSWER: B (because of the context clue: active)

1. The grocery store owner **exploits** the workers by underpaying

   them. _____

   A) abuses B) helps C) supports D) cares

2. Dr. London said we are **presumed** innocent until we are proven

   guilty. _____

   A) pleasure B) true C) assumed D) fact

3. Antoine offered his **condolences** to Alec when he found out Zarick

   almost beat him up. _____

   A) noise B) loud C) happy D) sympathy

4. The **generous** woman gave one million dollars to the church.

   _____

   A) dangerous B) giving C) selfish D) stingy

5. Tyrod was **infamous** because he bullied so many people. _____

   A) dishonorable B) kind C) right D) sweet

6. The coach **bellowed** when the karate kid hurt another kid on purpose. _____

   A) shouted B) cheered C) clapped D) cried

7. You must have **permission** from your parents to go on the school field trip. _____

   A) commands B) believe C) consent D) protection

8. The student could not hide his **delight** when he did well on the CRCT test. _____

   A) anger B) happiness C) sadness D) rage

9. Alec put himself in a **precarious** position when he lied to Dr. Richardson. _____

   A) harmless   B) comfortable C) safe D) dangerous

10. The story Morgan told me to read was hard to **comprehend**.

    _____

    A) understand B) forget C) overlook D) confused

Pre-Algebra Computations

Direction: Find the answers for X in the following problems.

Always use the opposite sign from the one in the problem you are solving. For example, in a multiplication problem, you must use division to find the value of X.

Example: x + 7 = 12

In this example, X is one side of an addition problem. To find the value of X in an addition problem, subtract the number on the opposite side of the addition problem (7) from the answer (12).

Solution:

X + 7 = 12

X = 12 − 7

X = 5

(1) 8 + x = 16 ; x = _____

(2) x − 12 = 20; x = _____

(3) 6 * x = 36 ; x = _____

(4) x / 12 = 2 ; x = _____

(5) 7 + x = 10 ; x = _____

(6) x − 8 = 15; x = _____

(7) 9 * x = 45 ; x = _____

(8) x / 11 = 4 ; x = _____

(9) x + 12 = 22 ; x = _____

(10) 14 − x = 6; x = _____

Teach Me, Coach: Karate
Karate Basic Terms

Listed below are basic terms that can be used in different phrases when talking about karate. Enjoy learning about the sport and remember it is never to be used to harm anyone, but only for sport and for self-defense.

Age (ah-gay): rising.

Anza (ah-n-zah): cross leg sitting.

Ate (ah-tay): smash.

Atemi (ah-tay-mee): concentrated destructive power.

Barai (bah-rye): to parry.

Bu (boo): military.

Budo (boo-doe): military way or way of fighting (examples: Judo, Kendo, Kyudo, Karate-do, Kobudo).

Budoka (boo-doe-kha): military art practitioner.

Chikara (chee-kha-rha): strength.

Chudan (chew-dahn): middle (examples: chest and stomach area).

Chuden (chew-den): intermediate level of instruction. Usually when pertaining to bunkai instruction.

Do (doe): way.

Genki (gehn-key): vigor; energy.

Hajime (ha-gee-may): begin.

Hanshi (hahn-shee): "Master." An honorary title given to the highest Black Belt of an organization, signifying their understanding of their art.

Hidari (he-dah-ray): left.

Ju (joo): flexibility.

Kamae (kah-may): fighting posture.

Kan (con): house or hall.

Karategi (kah-rah-teh-gee): a uniform.

Karateka (kah-rah-teh-kah): Someone who practices karate.

Kenpo (kem-po) or **Kempo** (kem-po): "Law of the Fist"

Ki (key) or **Qi** (key): intrinsic energy, a hidden strength that everyone possesses.

Kiai (kee-ii): "spirit joining."

Kobudo (ko-boo-doe): weapons.

Koshi (ko-she): ball of the foot.

Kumite (koo-me-tay): fighting.

Kuzushi (koo-zoo-she): to unbalance.

Kyu (kuu): the rank under black belt.

Kyusho (kuu-show): striking point, vital point.

Maai (mah-aye): distancing.

Mawate (may-wah-tay): turn.

Mokuso (mok-so): meditate.

Muchimi (moo-chee-me): To "stick" or "adhere" to an opponent without actually grabbing. Muchimi is mostly done with the forearms, though other parts of the body (in particular, the legs) are also used.

Obi (o-be): belt.

Okinawa Te (o-key-nah-wah tay): the original Okinawa fist art.

Okuden (oh-koo-den): "Secret Teaching". Usually used in relation to instruction in bunkai.

Rei (ray): formal bowing.

Reigi Zaho (ray-gee zah-hoe): courtesy or manners.

Renshu (rin-shoe): to train, practice, drill, etc.

Ryu (roo): school.

Ryu-ha (roo-ha): style.

Senpai (sin-pie): senior student.

Sensei (sin-say): teacher or "those who have gone before."

Shihan (shee-hahn): "teacher of teachers" senior instructor or dojo director.

Shinki (sheen-key): nerve.

Shita (she-tah): down.

Shoden (show-den): basic level of instruction. Usually used in relation to instruction in bunkai.

Skashi (skah-she): to avoid.

Suigetsu (see-gets): solar plexus.

Tachimas (tah-key-mahs): to rise or stand up.

Tai Sabaki (tie sah-bah-key): body movement.

Tori (toe-ree): a term given to the "aggressor" when working with a partner.

Tuite (too-it-tay): grappling techniques.

Ude (oo-day): forearm.

Uke (oo-key): a term given to the "defender" when working with a partner.

Ukemi (oo-kee-me): break fall.

Uye (oo-ee): up.

Waza (wah-zah): technique.

Yame (yah-may): stop.

Yoi (yoo-ee): command given to stand in ready stance.

Za Rei (zah ray): kneeling bow.

Okay, so now that you know many karate terms, go, train, and enjoy the martial arts form.

1) What is the word for *stop*? _____

2) The word *skashi* means _____.

3) What word means *school*? _____

4) The word *maai* means _____.

5) What does the word *do* mean?_____.

Answers: 1) Yame, 2) to avoid, 3) Ryu, 4) distancing, 5) way

Chapter 1 Solution

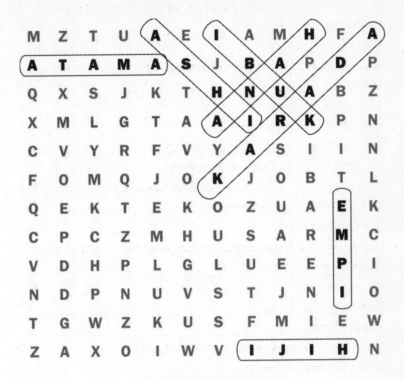

Atama (ah-tah-mah): head
Ashi (ah-she): foot and/or leg
Empi (em-pee): elbow
Hana (hah-nah): nose
Hiji (he-gee): elbow
Karada (kah-rah-dah): body
Kubi (koo-bee): neck

Chapter 2 Solution

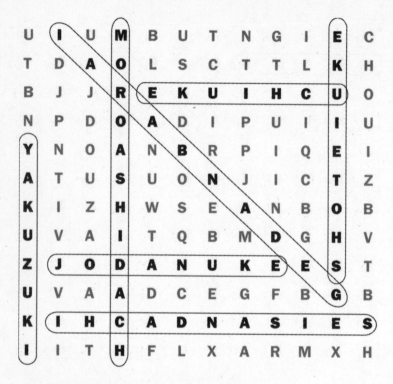

Gedan Barai (geh-dahn bah-rye): downward block
Jodan Uke (jo-dahn oo-key): upward block
Moro Ashi Dach (moor-oh aah-she dah-chee): fighting stance
Seisan Dachi (say-san dah-chee): forward stance
Shotei Uke (sho-tye oo-key): palm/heel block
Uchi Uke (oo-chee oo-key): inward block
Yaku Zuki (ya-koo zoo-key): reverse punch

Chapter 3 Solution

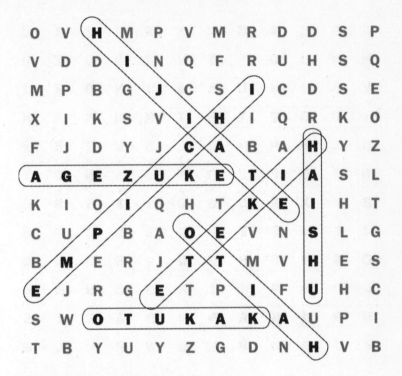

Age Zuke (ah-geh zoo-key): rising punch
Empi Uchi (em-pee oo-chee): elbow strike
Haishu (hi-shoo): back of hand
Haito (hi-toe): knife hand
Hiji Ate (he-gee ah-tay): elbow smash
Hike Te (hee-key tay): withdrawing hand; the hand on the hip
Kakuto (kah-koo-toe): bent wrist

Chapter 4 Solution

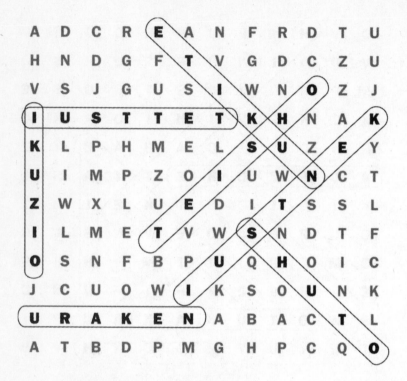

Kentsui (ken-t-sue-ee): hammer fist
Nukite (noo-key-tay): spear hand
Oi Zuki (oh-ee zoo-key): lunge punch
Shuto (shoo-toe): knife hand
Teisho (tay-show) or Shotei (show-tay): palm heel
Tettsui (tay-t-sue-ee): hammer fist
Uraken (ree-kin): back fist

Chapter 5 Solution

Age Uke (Ah-geh oo-key): upward block
Chudan Uke (chew-dahn oo-key): outward middle forearm block
Gedan Barai (geh-dahn bah-rye): downward block
Hasami Uke (ha-sah-may oo-key): scissor block
Jodan Uke (jo-dahn oo-key): upward block
Kosa Uke (co-sah oo-key): cross block
Shuto Uke (shoo-toh oo-key: knife hand block

Chapter 6 Solution

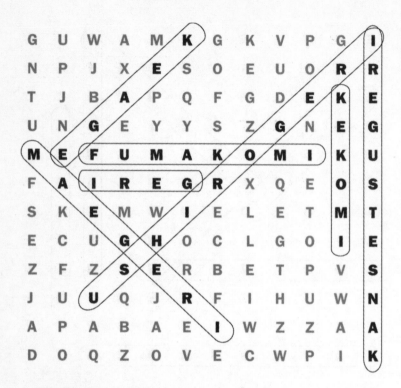

Geri (geh-rhee): kick
Fumakomi (foo-mah-ko-mee): side stomp kick
Kansetsu Geri (can-set-sue geh-rhee): kicks aimed at joints
Keage (key-ah-gay): snap
Kekomi (key-ko-mee): thrust
Mae Geri (mah-eh geh-rhee): front kick
Ushiro Geri (oo-she-row geh-rhee): back kick

Chapter 7 Solution

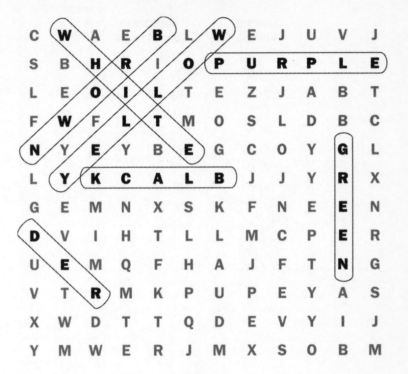

White
Yellow
Green
Purple
Brown
Black
Red

Answer Keys

Context Clues

1) A
2) C
3) D
4) B
5) A
6) A
7) C
8) B
9) D
10) A

Pre-Algebra Computations

1) 8
2) 32
3) 6
4) 24
5) 3
6) 23
7) 5
8) 44
9) 0
10) 8

ACKNOWLEDGMENTS

We get a kick out of debating in the Moore home. All have an opinion, and all love winning their case. However, in order to win at anything, you first must believe you can.

You can't win an argument if you don't believe in the facts. You can't win a sporting event if you feel inferior. And you can't win in life if you think you are not worthy of being a champion. The Lord wants you to believe in yourself and believe in His love for you. When you know you were perfectly and wonderfully made and that God is on your side—you can win any battle. Our prayer is that this book blesses everyone who reads it.

We have many to thank. Starting with our dear friends, Antonio and Gloria London and their family, especially nephew Jay, who inspired us with the character's last name and personality.

For our parents, Dr. Franklin and Shirley Perry, and Ann Redding, we win daily because of our God-fearing upbringing. Thank you for your enduring love.

For our Moody/Lift Every Voice Team, especially Roslyn Jordan, we win with getting the word out about this series because of your great efforts. Thank you for thinking out of the box with marketing our books.

For our Georgia Tech Fellowship of Christian Athletes supporters, especially Stephen and Charlotte Jensen, we win at ministering to others because of your support. Thank you for giving so much so that the Word could go forth.

For our assistant Alyxandra Pinkston, we win at getting our job done because you are there. Thank you for working so hard.

For our friends, who are dear to our hearts, Calvin Johnson and family, Tashard Choice, Chett and Lakeba Williams, Dennis and Leslie Perry, Clayton and Kelly Ivey, Jay and Debbie Spencer, Randy Roberts, John Rainey, Peyton Day, Jim and Deen Sanders, Paul and Susan Johnson, Bobby and Sarah Lundy, Sid Callaway, Dicky Clark, Danny Buggs, Chan and Laurie Gailey, Patrick and Krista Nix, Byron and Kim Johnson, Chris and Jenell Clark, Carol Hardy, Sid Callaway, Nicole Smith, Jackie Dixon, Harry and Torian Colon, Byron and Kim Forest, Vickie Davis, Brock White, Jamell Meeks, Michele Jenkins, Christine Nixon, Lois Barney, Veronica Evans, Sophia Nelson, Laurie Weaver, Byrant and Taiwanna Brown-Bolds, Deborah Thomas, Yolanda Rodgers-Howsie, Dayna Fleming, Denise Gilmore, Thelma Day, Adrian Davis, Donald and Deborah Bradley, and Walter and Marjorie Kimbrough, we win at having meaningful relationships because you care for us so dearly. Thank you for loving us.

For our children, Dustyn (who helped write the paper on page 119), Sydni, and Sheldyn, we win at being full because we are your parents. Thank you for being awesome young people who love God first.

For our new young readers, we win at making a difference in life because you've given this book a try. Thank you for embracing the message of this book.

And, for our heavenly Father, we win because we have You to daily see us through. Thank You for battling for us.

ALEC LONDON SERIES

978-0-8024-0411-4

978-0-8024-0410-7

978-0-8024-0412-1   978-0-8024-0414-5   978-0-8024-0413-8

The Alec London books are chapter books written for boys, 8–12 years old. Alec London is introduced in Stephanie Perry Moore's previously released series Morgan Love. In this new series, readers get a glimpse of Alec's life up close and personal. The series provides moral lessons that will aid in character development, teaching boys how to effectively deal with the various issues they face at this stage of life. The books will also help boys develop their English and math skills as they read through the stories and complete the entertaining and educational exercises provided at the end of each chapter and in the back of the book.

L E V B
LIFT EVERY VOICE BOOKS

LiftEveryVoiceBooks.com
MoodyPublishers.com

ALSO RANS SERIES

The Also Rans series is written for boys, ages 8-12. This series enourages youth, especially young boys, to give all they got in everything they do and never give up.

978-0-8024-2253-8

RUN, JEREMIAH, RUN

As a foster child, life for Jeremiah is a garbage bag filled with his things, a new school, and worst of all, finding a new family. Jeremiah holds on to his grandmother's promise of a handful of mustard seeds being planted one day to grow into a tree of his own. After being expelled from school again, he thinks that no one will want him to be a part of their family. With the help of his friends, he learns about teamwork and what it means to persevere.

978-0-8024-2259-0

COMING ACROSS JORDAN

When Jordan and brother Kevin decide to paint a mural (which is really graffiti) on the school's property, they get in trouble. They learn, along with their good friend Melanie, the lesson that even in using their talents to do something good, they have to pay attention and not break the rules.

L E V B
LIFT EVERY VOICE BOOKS

LiftEveryVoiceBooks.com
MoodyPublishers.com

MORGAN LOVE SERIES

978-0-8024-2263-7

978-0-8024-2264-4

978-0-8024-2267-5   978-0-8024-2266-8   978-0-8024-2265-1

The Morgan Love series is a chapter book series written for girls, 7–9 years old. The books provide moral lessons that will aid in character development. They will also help young girls develop their vocabulary, English, and math skills as they read through the stories and complete the entertaining and educational exercises provided at the end of each chapter and in the back of the book.

L E V B
LIFT EVERY VOICE BOOKS

LiftEveryVoiceBooks.com
MoodyPublishers.com

Lift Every Voice Books

Lift every voice and sing
Till earth and heaven ring,
Ring with the harmonies of Liberty;
Let our rejoicing rise
High as the listening skies,
Let it resound loud as the rolling sea.
Sing a song full of the faith that the dark past has taught us,
Sing a song full of the hope that the present has brought us,
Facing the rising sun of our new day begun
Let us march on till victory is won.

The Black National Anthem, written by James Weldon Johnson in 1900, captures the essence of Lift Every Voice Books. Lift Every Voice Books is an imprint of Moody Publishers that celebrates a rich culture and great heritage of faith, based on the foundation of eternal truth—God's Word. We endeavor to restore the fabric of the African-American soul and reclaim the indomitable spirit that kept our forefathers true to God in spite of insurmountable odds.

We are Lift Every Voice Books—Christ-centered books and resources for restoring the African-American soul.

For more information on other books and products
written and produced from a biblical perspective, go to
www.lifteveryvoicebooks.com or write to:

Lift Every Voice Books
820 N. LaSalle Boulevard
Chicago, IL 60610
www.lifteveryvoicebooks.com